GOOSEBUMPS HorrorLand™
ALL-NEW! ALL-TERRIFYING!
Also Available on Audiobook from Scholastic Audiobooks

GOOSEBUMPS®
NOW WITH BONUS FEATURES!
LOOK IN THE BACK OF THE BOOK
FOR EXCLUSIVE AUTHOR INTERVIEWS AND MORE.

ESCAPE FROM HORRORLAND

R.L. STINE

SCHOLASTIC INC.
New York Toronto London Auckland
Sydney Mexico City New Delhi Hong Kong

No part of this publication may be reproduced, stored in a retrieval system, or transmitted in any form or by any means, electronic, mechanical, photocopying, recording, or otherwise, without written permission of the publisher. For information regarding permission, write to Scholastic Inc., Attention: Permissions Department, 557 Broadway, New York, NY 10012.

ISBN 978-0-439-91879-4

Goosebumps book series created by Parachute Press, Inc.

Goosebumps HorrorLand #11: *Escape from HorrorLand*
copyright © 2009 by Scholastic Inc.

All rights reserved. Published by Scholastic Inc., *Publishers since 1920.* SCHOLASTIC, GOOSEBUMPS, GOOSEBUMPS HORRORLAND, and associated logos are trademarks and/or registered trademarks of Scholastic Inc.

12   11   10   9   8   7   6   5   11   12   13   14/0

Printed in the U.S.A.
First printing, June 2009

ESCAPE FROM HORRORLAND

1

Six kids formed a circle around my brother, Luke, and me. Their fists were clenched tight. And their eyes were shooting darts at us.

I know, I know. That's a strange way to start my story. But *everything* is strange in HorrorLand. Luke and I had just met these kids — and they were already angry at us.

My name is Lizzy Morris. I'm thirteen and Luke is eleven.

Luke and I were in HorrorLand a year ago. We had plenty of scary adventures. Then, a few months ago, we learned that something was very wrong at the park.

One of the Horrors, a park worker, began to send us mysterious e-mails. He told us about a group of kids who were in big trouble.

We started studying the park, and we wrote a blog about what we learned.

We found out that fourteen kids had been invited to spend a free week as Very Special

Guests. And when they arrived, things turned out to be way TOO scary!

Now the kids believed their lives were in danger. Someone was trying to *scare* them to death! They were desperate to escape HorrorLand.

These kids discovered that another park existed — a place called Panic Park. It could be reached only by traveling through mirrors.

I know it sounds crazy, but stick with me. Eight kids had already escaped to Panic Park. They all believed they'd be safer there.

And now the remaining six kids were unhappy with Luke and me because we had a warning for them: *Don't go there!*

I didn't blame them for being suspicious. I mean, Luke and I knew all the kids' names because we'd been studying them. But the kids had never seen us before.

And here we were, warning them *not* to go to Panic Park.

Their eyes narrowed at us. Their faces turned hard and cold. "Who are you? Why are you trying to trick us?" Matt Daniels asked.

He was athletic looking and tall. Matt and Carly Beth Caldwell appeared to be the leaders of the group. She was cute — short and pixieish. She looked a lot younger than twelve.

"We're not tricking you," Luke said. "We're trying to help you."

"We've been studying both parks," I said. "We've done a lot of research. We think you are safer in HorrorLand."

"You're both spies for the Horrors!" Robby Schwartz cried. "We *know* we're not safe in HorrorLand."

"Who are you working for?" Jackson Gerard demanded. His twin sister, Jillian, glared at us, scowling. They were both tall and thin, with straight brown hair and dark eyes.

"Are you working for that maniac superhero? The one who calls himself The Keeper?" Jackson said. "He's trying to keep us here, too."

"We — we're not working for anyone," I stammered. "I told you — Luke and I have found a lot of information. We think Panic Park is a big trap."

Some kids snickered and groaned. Carly Beth rolled her eyes. "Can you prove it?" she asked.

"Well . . . no," I said. "But —"

"Eight of our friends are already there," Matt said. "Are you telling us they walked into a trap?"

"If it's true, we *definitely* have to follow them there," Julie Martin said. "To help rescue them."

The afternoon sun sat high above the trees. We were standing on the shore of the Black Lagoon. I could hear the howls from Wolfsbane Forest, which stretched out to my right.

Robby glanced from side to side. "We have to hurry," he said. "The Horrors are searching for us. We can't stand here arguing with two kids we don't know."

"But . . . Luke and I are trying to help," I insisted.

Jillian stepped up close to me. Her eyes burned into mine. After a long, tense moment, she turned to the others.

"I read Lizzy's mind," Jillian said. "We can't listen to her. She's lying."

"Huh?" I let out a gasp. "No *way*! I'm NOT!" I cried.

"She's definitely lying," Jillian told them.

I swallowed hard. My mouth suddenly felt dry. My hands were shaking. "You — you can read minds?" I stammered.

Jillian sneered at me. "My brother and I have special powers," she said. "I read your thoughts, Lizzy. I know you're not telling the truth. You must be working for the Horrors."

And that's when the six kids surrounded Luke and me.

"I AM telling the truth!" I screamed. "We are NOT working for the Horrors."

I could see they were desperate. And frightened.

And angry.

They closed in on us. "I *swear* I'm telling the truth!" I cried. "Don't hurt us! HEY — don't hurt us!"

Matt grabbed my brother by the shoulders. "You don't want to be on my bad list," he growled.

"Down, boy!" Luke said. "I'm your *friend*. Lizzy and I —"

"We know things about Panic Park!" I shouted. "Things you don't know."

The kids glared angrily at us. I could feel the tension in the air. Matt held on to Luke's shoulders.

"She's lying," Jillian insisted. "I'm reading her thoughts. I can't tell *why* she's lying. I just know she is."

"Give me a chance!" I cried. "Let me tell you one thing about Panic Park — okay?"

"Go ahead," Carly Beth said. "One thing."

"The park doesn't exist!" I said.

A short silence. Then they laughed.

"You're totally crazy!" Jackson said.

Julie squinted at me. "If Panic Park doesn't exist, how did eight of our friends travel there?"

"Enough!" Matt shouted. "Everyone shut up! We can't stand here talking. These two kids are trying to keep us here so the Horrors can catch us."

Matt lifted Luke off the ground.

Luke tried to kick him. But Matt was too strong.

"Let me down! Hey — give me a break!" Luke cried.

Julie, Jackson, and Carly Beth stepped up to me. Their faces were angry and threatening. "Tell us why you're here," Jackson demanded.

Before I could answer, they let out a shout.

We all turned to see a tall Horror come running out of the shadows. He was waving his big paws above his head as he ran.

Carly Beth gasped. Her face went pale.

"We're caught!" Matt cried. He let my brother drop to the ground. "They've found us!"

Kids turned to run — then stopped.

"Byron!" Robby Schwartz shouted. "Hey, I don't believe it! It's Byron."

The Horror was big and strong looking. He wore green overalls over his purple fur. The short yellow horns on top of his head caught the afternoon sunlight. His eyes kept darting from side to side.

"Byron — where have you been?" Matt stepped up to the big Horror.

"What's going on?" Jillian asked.

7

"No time," Byron replied, his big chest heaving. "You're all okay? Did the others escape to Panic Park?"

"They're gone," Matt said. "We tried to follow them. But —"

"You don't have much time," Byron said. "The other Horrors are searching every inch of HorrorLand to find you. I'm the only one on your side. They're very angry. Believe me, you don't want them to catch you."

"What do we do?" Carly Beth asked. "Can you get us out of here?"

Byron didn't answer her. He was staring at Luke and me. "Who are you?" he demanded. "You're not Very Special Guests."

"We . . . we want to help these kids," I stammered.

"We think they're working for the Horrors," Jackson told Byron. "They're trying to keep us here."

"We're not working for *anyone*," I said. "We know some things about Panic Park. We don't think it's safe."

Byron shook his head. "You're wrong," he said. "Come with me. You'll find out soon enough what's safe and what isn't safe."

He gazed all around. Then he motioned for everyone to follow him.

"Where are we going?" Matt asked.

"I think I can get you out of here," Byron replied. And then he added, "If we're quick."

Jackson hurried to catch up to Byron. "But why are you bringing Lizzy and Luke?" he asked. "We don't want them with us."

"Take them with you," Byron said. "Better to keep them close."

"But . . . but . . ." I sputtered. "Luke and I are on YOUR side!"

I could see that no one believed me.

"No problem. I'll keep them close," Jillian said. "And I'll read their minds. We'll know what these two are *really* thinking."

A chill rolled down my back. I felt so strange. These kids didn't know Luke and me. But they didn't trust us — and they didn't like us.

We have to prove ourselves to them, I thought. *But — how?*

The sun was still high above the trees. For some reason, the park had closed early that day. No one around. Food carts stood empty across Zombie Plaza.

The rides had all stopped. The music had been turned off. No voices anywhere. Just a deep, creepy silence — and the thud of our shoes on the pavement.

We trotted behind Byron past the carnival games area. I saw a Horror at the Head Toss game. He was setting his real-looking human heads on a shelf. He didn't turn around as we jogged past.

Byron stopped suddenly and turned. He led us along the back of the games — to a tiny black building at the end of the path. The building had a single door and a flat roof. No sign.

We huddled in front of the door. No one said a word.

Did this little building really lead to Panic Park?

Byron grabbed the door handle and twisted it. "Locked," he said. "No problem."

He turned to Matt. "Use your key card. The Panic Park key card I gave you when you first arrived."

Matt fumbled in his jeans pocket. He pulled out a gray plastic card.

"Hurry," Byron urged. "They'll be coming for you. I know they will."

Matt gripped the plastic card and shoved it into a tiny slot on the side of the door. He grabbed the knob and turned it.

He pushed the door open.

Dark inside. I couldn't see a thing.

"Hurry. Get in. Get in!" Byron said in a whisper. He gave Matt a gentle shove.

We scrambled inside. Down a narrow aisle.

So dark in there. The only light came from the open doorway.

What *was* this place?

I waited for my eyes to adjust.

Slowly, the room came into focus — and I gasped in surprise.

3

"Mirrors!" Carly Beth exclaimed. Her shoulder bumped me as she leaned toward the glass. "It's a Hall of Mirrors."

"But that's impossible!" Robby's voice cried out in the darkness. "There are no mirrors in HorrorLand."

We were all jammed tight together. Standing in a narrow aisle between two long rows of mirrors.

The air felt hot and damp. A trickle of sweat ran down my forehead.

Our reflections stared back at us. Shadowy reflections. Wide-eyed faces staring out at us in surprise.

Luke did a little dance. "Look — there's a *hundred* of me! The reflections just keep going."

"Byron, how did this get here?" Carly Beth asked.

"These mirrors weren't here before — were they?" Julie asked.

12

"Byron?"

We turned, squinting into the sunlight from the open door.

"He's gone," I said. "He left us. We're on our own."

"Why did he leave us here without saying a word?" Carly Beth asked.

"Don't chicken out now," Matt said. "Byron got us this far. We have to go the rest of the way."

"Yeah. We know what to do," Jackson agreed. "These mirrors will take us to Panic Park."

Luke pushed up against me. He raised his mouth to my ear. "Lizzy, they're making a big mistake," he whispered.

"*Shhhhh.*" I pressed my finger over Luke's lips. "Don't say a word. We don't really know what's in the other park," I whispered.

"But, Lizzy —"

"They all think they'll be safer there," I told him. "That Horror Byron thinks so, too. If we speak up, they won't let us help them."

Carly Beth raised her hand to the mirror. I saw her fingers sink right into the glass.

"It's . . . soft," she murmured. "The glass is soft. Like Jell-O."

"Everyone take a deep breath," Matt said. "We're going in. We're going into the glass." His voice cracked.

He was one of the bravest in the group. But I could see that Matt was just as scared as I was.

13

"Panic Park, here we come!" Jackson shouted.

He lurched forward. His head disappeared into the glass. The rest of his body moved into it.

I could see him in the mirror. I watched until his body grew smaller and smaller, and he disappeared into the distance.

Carly Beth went next. She ducked her head and shoved her hands forward and stepped into the liquid glass.

I turned to Luke. He had his hands shoved deep in his jeans pockets. He was chewing his bottom lip as he gazed into the mirror in front of him.

"Lizzy, are we . . . are we really doing this?" he asked in a tiny voice.

"Yes," I said. *"Now!"*

"But . . . will we ever find our way back?" Luke asked.

The question sent a shiver down my spine. I didn't know how to answer it.

I grabbed Luke's hand, and we stepped into the mirror.

4

"Hey!" I uttered a cry as my face sank into the soft glass.

Much colder than I expected. My cheeks tingled. I felt the cold goo wrap around my head, my hair.

I took a step. Then another. I had to push hard. It was like moving through frozen foam rubber.

My chest started to ache. I realized I was holding my breath. I let the air out in a long *whoosh*.

Could I breathe in this thick goo?

I sucked in a tiny bit of air. Then a little more. The air froze my nostrils.

Stretching my hands out in front of me, I took another step.

So dark in here. And so cold. The goo wrapped around me tightly. As if I were packed in snow.

I turned to my brother. "Luke?"

My voice sounded hollow, muffled by the liquid glass.

"Luke? Are you there?"

15

I couldn't see him. Too dark. I couldn't see anything.

I forced myself forward. I tried not to breathe. The frozen air burned my nose.

My whole body shivered. I moved slowly through the darkness, listening for Luke . . . for the others.

But I was surrounded by a heavy, terrifying silence.

Another step. My legs were trembling.

It's like walking through a nightmare, I thought. *Like walking along the bottom of the ocean.*

All alone . . . all alone.

Would it ever end?

Then — something grabbed my hand.

Something pulled me hard.

I opened my mouth to scream. But no sound came out.

And I went falling . . . falling into the thick darkness.

I felt a *whoosh* of warm air.

The heavy goo fell away from me as I stumbled forward.

The blackness lifted to gray. I could see. I could see who was pulling me out of the mirror.

Luke!

He gave my hand one last tug, and I stumbled onto the floor.

Blinking, I tried to force my eyes to adjust to the dim light.

"Lizzy, are you okay?" Luke's voice rang in my ears. I couldn't shake off the deep silence.

"I . . . I guess," I choked out.

I glanced around. The two rows of mirrors came into focus.

Were we back where we started?

Matt came staggering out of a mirror. He grabbed Jillian to catch his balance. Julie shook her head hard, as if trying to shake the goo from her hair.

Luke laughed, a shrill, nervous laugh. "That was totally WEIRD!" he cried.

"We're back in the Hall of Mirrors," Robby said. "Did we do something wrong?"

Matt shoved past me, along the row of mirrors to the door. He pushed the door open and peered out.

"Oh, wow," he said. "I totally don't believe this. Check it out."

We all stampeded to the door. A gust of fresh air felt good on my face.

I squeezed outside along with the other kids. I knew instantly we were in a different park.

I saw a Ferris wheel in the distance. A steep roller coaster beside it.

A tent stood in a wide, grassy park. The flap was open, and I could see an old-fashioned ride with white wooden swans inside.

"We . . . we made it!" Carly Beth cried. "This must be the other park!"

"Panic Park," Julie murmured. "Do you believe it? We're in Panic Park!"

I rubbed my eyes. "Why is everything in black and white?" I asked.

No one answered. We all huddled near the door to the Hall of Mirrors and gazed around.

I could see only shades of gray. The tent. The grass. The trees. The rides in the distance.

"It's all so drab," Robby said. "Like the color has been washed out."

I gasped as a group of people walked by.

"Look!" Luke cried. "They're in black and white, too!"

I suddenly realized the park was crowded. A long line of people stood outside the tent to the swan ride. Small groups of people moved back and forth in front of us.

All shades of gray. No color. No color anywhere. Their clothes were weird. Old-fashioned.

None of them turned to look at us. We were still our normal colors. But no one seemed to notice.

"Totally weird," Carly Beth muttered. "It's like we stepped into an old black-and-white movie."

"Let's get going," Matt said. "We've got to find the other kids."

"Yeah. Maybe they know what's up with this weird place," Robby said.

"At least we're safe," Jillian said. "We're out of HorrorLand."

She turned and stared at me. She expected me to argue with her.

But I didn't say anything. I started walking, following Matt and Carly Beth, who led the way.

We passed the swan ride tent. Behind it, the path led to a row of white buildings with black doors.

Shadowy, gray people stood in a long line in front of a building with a grinning skull on the front. A black-and-white sign proclaimed: SCREAM HOUSE.

Next to it, people stood in a circle, peering down into a deep, black pit. The sign in front of it read: HOLE OF HORROR.

"This park is *huge*," Julie murmured. "How will we ever find the other kids?"

"I have an idea," I said.

Jillian sneered at me. "You want to go back to HorrorLand and forget about them, right?"

"No way," I said. "Give me a break. I'm trying to help."

"You can help by going away," Jillian snapped. "We know you and your brother are spies for the Horrors."

"Not true," I said. "I swear. You're wrong, Jillian. You're totally wrong about us."

I saw a little girl walking by herself. I hurried over to her.

The girl wore a gray skirt and a gray blouse. Her long, wavy hair was black. Her face was pale gray.

When she raised her eyes to me, I could see the sadness on her face. Her eyes were ringed with black circles. Her gray cheeks were puffy and tearstained.

I bent down to talk to her. "Have you seen eight kids, all walking together?" I asked.

Her chin trembled. She spoke in a tiny mouse

voice, so soft I could barely hear her. "I vanished," she said.

My mouth dropped open. "What did you say?"

"I vanished," the little girl repeated. "I vanished. Can you find me?"

The other kids gathered around us.

"Has she seen our friends?" Julie asked.

"I . . . I don't know," I stammered. I turned back to the little girl. "Are you lost?" I asked.

The little gray girl stared up at me with her sad, dark eyes. "Can you find me?" she whispered. "I vanished. I vanished. I vanished. Can you find me?"

Gray tears trickled down her pale cheeks.

I reached out. I tried to put my hand on her shoulder —

— and my hand *went right through* the little girl!

I let out a gasp. I staggered back, away from the girl.

Her tears carved dark lines in her pale cheeks. Her slender shoulders sagged. "Please find me," she whispered. "I vanished. Please find me."

"I . . . I'll try," I said.

I didn't know what else to say.

Jillian stepped forward. She gazed down on the shadowy little girl. "I'm trying to read her mind," she said. "But I'm getting only static. It's like . . . the signal is too weak . . . too far away."

A young man and woman stepped up behind the little girl. They wore black T-shirts and black shorts. Their skin was the color of ashes after a fire dies out.

"We all vanished," the woman said. Her gray eyes were blank, like clear glass.

"We all vanished when the park disappeared,"

the man said. "We are the shadows. We are the shadow people."

"I don't understand you," I said. "Shadows? What are you saying?"

"We're all that's left," the man said. His voice sounded muffled, far away. "The park disappeared, and we did, too."

"Find me," the little girl repeated. "Find me. Can you find me?"

"You mean — you're DEAD?" Matt asked.

"No. We're what's left," the woman said. "We're the shadows we left behind when we disappeared. Don't you see?"

"We . . . don't understand!" Matt cried.

More shadowy, black-and-white people arrived. Little boys and girls and their parents. A few gray, sad-looking teenagers.

"I vanished," the little girl said. She began to sob. Her whole body shook. "Can't you find me? Can't you find me *anywhere*?"

The shade people formed a circle around us. They began to move around and around us. Their low voices were chilling as they murmured to us.

"We're all that's left."

"Where did we go?"

"Can you find us?"

"I vanished. Please find me."

"I'm a shade now. We're all shades. It's so drab and dark here."

"Where did we go?"

Muttering their sad words, they circled us faster and faster — until they were a moaning blur of charcoal gray.

"Find us! Find us!"

"Don't leave us here!"

"We can't let you leave till you find us!"

"Let's get out of here!" Carly Beth screamed.

We took off running.

I ducked my head — and ran right into the swirling shadow people.

I felt a shudder of cold, as if I were breaking through solid ice.

And then I was on the other side, outside the twirling circle of gray. Outside the wailing voices.

The others came bursting out, and we kept running until the voices faded behind us.

A strong gust of wind blew hard against us. I heard a *smaaaack* sound.

Robby let out a startled cry. I turned and saw him struggling to pull crinkled newspaper pages off his face.

He unfolded them. "The wind carried this . . ." he started.

But then his eyes went wide as he read the front page — and he gasped in shock.

"Robby — what's wrong?" I cried.

He stared at the headline on the paper for a few seconds more. Then he held it up so we could all read it: **PANIC PARK CLOSED**.

I felt my throat tighten. Luke and I exchanged glances. My brother and I had a hunch about this. But we were never sure it was true.

Seeing the bold, black type of the headline sent a cold shudder down my back.

"What does it say?" Matt asked Robby. "Read the rest of it."

We huddled close as Robby read:

"'Following the disappearance of several park visitors, Panic Park was shut down forever today. This followed the strange deaths of many park visitors in the past year.

"'City officials announced that the park — all its rides and buildings — will be torn down immediately.'"

"But — the park is still here!" Matt said. "It hasn't been torn down. We're standing in it."

We all started talking at once.

"It must be a mistake."

"They probably changed their minds."

"Did it really say a lot of people died here? Those shadow people . . ."

"Wait . . . wait," Robby said, holding up one hand to quiet us. "There's more."

We fell silent. Why did Robby suddenly look so pale?

"Check out the date at the top of this newspaper," he said. He pointed to it with a trembling finger. "July 12, 1974."

No one said a word.

Another strong gust of wind lifted the newspaper out of Robby's hands. It swirled into the air and sailed across the plaza.

Carly Beth shook her head. "This is too frightening," she said. "Has Panic Park really been closed since 1974?"

"Does that mean we traveled back in time?" Robby said. "I've drawn a lot of comic strips about time travel. But it can't really happen. No way!"

"You can't travel through mirrors, either," Julie said. "But we did it. How can you be sure we didn't travel back to 1974? And now we're stuck here. Like . . . like prisoners."

"Maybe those shadow people told us the truth," Matt said. "Didn't they say they were here when the park closed?"

"And now they're *dead*?" Julie cried. "That little girl? The others? They've been *dead* since 1974?"

"This is too weird," Jillian said. "We have to stay calm. We can't be having all these crazy thoughts."

My mind was spinning. I had warned them about Panic Park. But they didn't want to believe me.

I decided I had to speak up. "I think we should go back to the Hall of Mirrors," I said. "I think we should go back to HorrorLand."

"Lizzy is right," my brother, Luke, quickly chimed in. "If we go back, we can find out the truth about Panic Park."

"No way!" Jackson cried. He glared at Luke and me. "No way! No way! You just want to leave the other kids here? We can't do that. We have to find them first!"

Jillian spoke up angrily, curling her fists at her sides. "Jackson is right. Our friends need us."

She turned to the others. "Lizzy and Luke don't care about them," she said. "They're not really part of our group. They showed up just as we were leaving HorrorLand and tried to stop us. Now they're trying to tell us what to do."

"I knew we *never* should have let them come with us," Jackson added.

It's a good thing I'm the calm one in my family. If I wasn't, I'd probably try to slug Jillian.

She had no right to accuse Luke and me that way.

I saw the angry look on Luke's face. He made a move toward Jackson. Luke is a foot shorter than Jackson! I grabbed him by the shoulders and held him back.

"Luke and I just want to help," I said quietly. "Let's find the rest of your friends and get out of here as fast as we can."

"She's right," Robby said. "Something is terribly wrong here. If the park really did close in 1974 . . ." His voice trailed off.

Julie had a camera strapped around her neck. She raised it and stared at it as if seeing it for the first time. "I almost forgot I had this," she said. "Let me take a quick photo of everyone. You know. Just for proof that we were here."

She waved us over to a tall sign. The sign was black with gray letters. It read: CAUTION. GHOUL CROSSING.

Julie lined us up in front of the sign. "I can't believe I forgot to take pictures," she said. "We'll all want them when we're home safe and sound — right?"

She moved Carly Beth and Luke to the front

row. They were the shortest. The rest of us stood in a line in front of the sign.

No one smiled.

I think we were all thinking about the newspaper. Had we walked into some kind of weird time warp?

Julie flashed the photo.

Then she raised the back of the camera and squinted at the viewscreen.

She brought the camera closer to her face. She squinted at it some more.

Then she let out a cry: "I don't *believe* it!"

Julie's hand shook so hard, she nearly dropped the camera.

I grabbed it and gazed at the viewscreen. "Whoa," I muttered. "Totally weird."

I could see the GHOUL CROSSING sign. But where were *we*?

None of us were in the picture. Just the sign. Black and gray. No color anywhere.

"Come on," Julie said, waving us back in place. "We need a do-over. It can't be the camera. This is my newest one."

We lined up again. Carly Beth and Luke stood in front. The rest of us huddled close behind them.

Julie raised the camera and gazed into the viewscreen. "Okay. I can see everyone clearly. Matt, squeeze in a little."

She took a step back. "Okay. I've got you all now. Don't anybody move."

She flashed the camera.

We hurried over to check it out with her.

"You . . . you're INVISIBLE!" Julie cried.

"That's *impossible*!" Matt said. He turned the back of the camera toward him to see it better. "Huh? Where ARE we?"

Robby shook his head. I could see him shiver.

"I . . . I wish I hadn't read so much science fiction," he said. "I wish I hadn't read so many comic books."

"Robby, what are you thinking?" Carly Beth demanded.

"Well . . ." He shivered again. "If we *did* go back in time, we wouldn't show up in a picture."

"Why not?" Jillian asked.

"Because we weren't born yet!" Robby replied. "None of us was *alive* in 1974!"

"Stop! This is giving me a headache!" Julie said.

"Why did you say that?" Luke said to Robby. "Now I am totally creeped out."

"Do you mean we're standing in this park that doesn't exist? And we aren't even BORN yet?" Matt cried.

Matt pointed across the plaza. "We should try to take a picture of one of those shadow people over there," he said.

We turned to stare at a group of shades walking around a fountain.

"Bet it wouldn't come out, either," Julie said.

"Let's stay away from those shades!" Luke said.

And then Carly Beth let out a cry. "Over there!" She pointed to a small, square building that looked like a log cabin.

A black-and-white sign over the door read: INFORMATION BOOTH.

"Come on," Carly Beth said, trotting toward the cabin. "Maybe someone is in there. Maybe someone can help us."

"Maybe . . ." I muttered. But I didn't really believe it.

My legs felt as if they weighed a thousand pounds as I jogged to the information booth. I knew it was my feeling of dread weighing me down.

I had the most frightening hunch that our troubles here were just beginning.

I followed the others through the open door. We stepped into a small, dark room. Gray light filtered in through a tiny window.

A black counter stretched across the back. Cobwebs hung down like a curtain from the low ceiling.

"Anyone here?" I called in a shaky voice. "Anyone in here? *Please?*"

"Check this out!" Matt said. He picked up something from a low black table. It looked like a magazine.

"It's the park guide," he said. He held it up. "It's in color!"

We gathered around. The cover was in bright reds and yellows.

Matt opened it. I looked over his shoulder. I saw photos of a flaming carousel. A tall blue-and-green roller coaster. A bright red food cart, selling Human Pancakes.

"What happened here?" Matt said, gazing around the dark cabin room. "Why has all the color in the park faded away?"

"Check out the clothes on that guy!" Julie said, pointing to a photo in the guidebook. "Are those bell-bottom pants?"

"That girl with him is wearing a miniskirt with white boots," Carly Beth said. "I saw outfits like that in my grandma's old photo album."

I saw an African-American man with a tall afro. Two guys next to him had long sideburns.

"How old is this guidebook?" Jillian asked.

"Three guesses," Matt said. "I'll bet you it's from 1974."

He pulled something out from the back of the book. "A map!" he said. He unfolded it carefully. "It's a map of the whole park. All in color."

"Maybe it will help us find the exit," I said.

Jillian rolled her eyes. "There you go again," she said. "Did you forget our friends, Lizzy? You just want to leave them here and get out of the park as fast as you can?"

"That's not what I meant," I said. "I just —"

"Whoa. Check this out," Robby called from across the room. He was leaning over the long counter. He waved to us. "There's someone behind the desk."

We hurried beside him. Sitting in a low chair was a wooden mannequin. A dummy. He wore jeans and a checked flannel shirt. He had a black baseball cap pulled over his head. A button on the cap read: GUIDE.

His wooden hands rested on the chair arms. The chair was tilted back. His eyes were closed, as if he were asleep.

I spotted a small sign behind him on the wall. I read it out loud: "'Push the button and Rocky will answer your question.'"

"Where's the button?" Carly Beth asked. "Quick — find the button."

I spotted a black button at the edge of the counter. I pushed it.

The dummy blinked. It raised its head. The head made a creaking sound as it leaned toward us.

The wooden mouth slowly opened. . . .

"Ohh, gross!" I cried.

I watched a fat worm curl out from the open mouth. Then another.

Worms poked out of the dummy's nostrils and dropped onto its lap. Another worm crawled out from its left eye.

"GO-O-O AWA-A-A-AY!" the dummy rasped in a scratchy recorded voice. It sounded like a crackling, old phonograph record.

"GO-O-O-O-O AWA-A-A-A-AY . . ."

Worms fell wetly from its nose and open mouth and plopped onto its lap.

I pushed the button again. "Can you help us?" I shouted.

"Can you help us find our friends?" Carly Beth asked.

"Please! Can you help us?" I asked.

"The park is CLOSED!" the dummy rasped. A big knot of worms plopped from its mouth. Worms curled out one nostril and into the other.

"The park is CLOSED! The park is CLOSED! The park is CLOSED! The park is CLOSED!"

35

10

I ran out of the cabin with my hands pressed over my ears. I couldn't stand that scratchy, hoarse voice. And I kept seeing the worms squirming out of the dummy's nose, mouth, and eye.

The park stretched in front of us in grays and blacks. The only color, besides us, was on the park guide that Matt clutched under his arm.

I heard a dry flapping sound. I looked up to see a flock of crows flying low overhead. The birds made ugly cawing sounds as they soared over us.

We all gathered at a clump of low benches shaped like coffins. I slumped down beside Luke and shut my eyes. I struggled to get the ugly dummy out of my thoughts.

Julie sat on a bench away from the rest of us, hugging herself. Matt and Carly Beth sat near me. They both stared at the shadow people moving silently back and forth along a fence in the distance.

"Okay, okay, we're all pretty freaked," Jackson said finally. He stared down at the ground as he spoke. Beside him, his twin sister, Jillian, had her eyes shut.

"I'm scared, too," Jackson said. "I've never been this scared. But we can't just try to escape without rescuing the others."

"If only we could find a living human," Carly Beth said. "Just one normal, living human. Someone we could talk to. But so far . . ." She didn't finish her sentence.

Robby sat down near Julie. He buried his face in his hands.

"Robby, what are you thinking about?" I asked.

He raised his head slowly. "Here's one more idea," he said. "It's all so totally unreal. But . . ."

He took a deep breath. "We got to Panic Park through mirrors — right? So . . . maybe we entered a mirror reality. A reality that's side by side with our world. You know. Like a parallel universe."

Jackson shook his head. "That's even crazier than going back in time."

"I can't follow that at all," Julie said. "I can understand going back in time. But a mirror reality? Whoa! Give me a break, Robby.

I think you've been reading comic books too long!"

"Maybe I can explain it to you, Julie, if I use tiny words," Robby snapped.

"Hey!" Matt jumped to his feet. "I don't know what to believe. But we've got to keep it together. Look. Our lives were in danger in HorrorLand, and we escaped — right? So we can do the same thing here."

"But how do we find the others?" Carly Beth asked. Her voice was high and shrill. She couldn't hide her fear. "How do we ever get back to our parents? To our homes?"

Her eyes narrowed. "Oh. Wait," she murmured.

She pulled her cell phone from her jeans pocket. "I'll try my phone. It didn't work in HorrorLand. They had it jammed or something. But maybe it'll work here. Maybe I can call home."

She flipped the phone open and pushed some numbers. Then she raised it to her ear — and SCREAMED.

11

The phone fell from Carly Beth's hand and clattered to the ground. She grabbed the sides of her head and shut her eyes. "It hurts . . ." she moaned.

I could hear the shrill squeal pouring out of her phone on the ground. It rose and fell like an ambulance siren.

Julie dropped down beside Carly Beth and put an arm around her shoulders. "Are you okay?"

Carly Beth blinked several times. "My head is still ringing," she murmured.

Robby pulled a cell phone from his pocket. He dialed a number. Then he held the phone away from him as far as he could reach.

We all heard the deafening screech.

"Okay. So our phones don't work," Matt said. "But we're making progress."

Robby stared at him. "Progress?"

"Yeah," Matt said. He held up the park map and the guidebook. "We have these."

He spread the map out on one of the coffin tops. "I just had an idea," he said. He turned to Carly Beth. "Remember where we saw Britney and Molly last?"

Carly Beth thought for a moment. "Sabrina and I had just arrived in HorrorLand," she said. "You showed us a tiny piece of mirror. I saw two girls in the mirror."

"Right," Matt said. "That was Britney and Molly. They vanished from HorrorLand before you arrived."

"Yes," Carly Beth said. "We saw them riding some kind of carousel. It had flames shooting out of it. Like the whole ride was on fire."

Matt leaned over the map. "Let's find the flaming carousel," he said. "Maybe the girls are still there, or somewhere nearby. Or maybe they left us a clue."

It didn't take long to find the carousel on the map. Matt stabbed his finger on the spot, very near the roller coaster.

"Let's go," he said. He folded up the map and tucked it into his back pocket.

We walked in silence along a high gray wall. A row of dark, empty shops stood across the path. I saw shadows in the doorways. The shadows moved. They turned as we passed by.

Shadow people watching from a distance. Always watching.

The wind felt cold and damp. It pushed against us as if trying to hold us back. We lowered our heads and moved through the gray park.

We passed low white buildings. Their doors were open, but I could see only blackness inside. A gray sign had fallen to the pavement. Most of it had rusted out, but I could read the words: GHOULS ONLY.

Shadow people floated in and out behind us. Were they following us?

Squinting through the gray, I saw a tall black Ferris wheel rise up in front of us. "Hey!" I cried out. "It's moving!"

"Weird," Carly Beth said, stopping to stare. "Who can be riding it?"

Matt pointed. "The flaming carousel should be right over there."

We began to walk faster. But a shout made us all stop.

"Hey! Guys! Guys! Up here!"

I glanced up. We were passing a tall fake mountain. It was maybe three or four stories high. The mountainside was rocky and had patches of fake snow all the way up.

A boy and a girl waved frantically to us from a cliff at the top of the mountain. "Hey! Matt! Carly Beth! Up here!"

They were both tall and very thin. They both had straight black hair. And even from down below, I could see the flash of their blue eyes.

"Billy!" Matt shouted. "Sheena! How did you get up there? Are the others up there with you?"

I don't think they could hear Matt. They kept waving and shouting. "Up here! Up here!"

Matt turned to the rest of us. "It's Billy and Sheena Deep."

He cupped his hands around his mouth and shouted, "We're coming! Don't move! We're coming to get you!"

A narrow path circled the mountain, heading toward the top. We all started to climb single file. The path was steep and hard and slippery, with patches of fake snow. Our shoes slid on the glassy surface.

"Oh!" I felt my shoes slide out from under me. Nothing to grab on to.

I fell forward. My knees banged down hard, and I started to slide.

My hands grabbed at the path. But it was as smooth as a playground slide. I couldn't stop myself. I slid all the way back to the bottom.

Luke turned. "Lizzy, are you okay?"

"Yeah. Fine," I grumbled. I leaned forward and started to climb again.

We were all about a third of the way up when I heard a deep rumbling sound.

I stopped. I didn't see anything.

The rumbling grew to a roar. The surface beneath me started to shake.

And then I saw it — *rocks*. Dozens of jagged, gigantic rocks! Roaring down the mountainside. Tumbling, bouncing hard and high.

Streaming down at us.

A rock slide!

"We — we're going to be CRUSHED!" I screamed. "BURIED alive!"

12

The roar of the falling rocks drowned out our screams.

I dropped to the hard surface and began tumbling down the mountainside. Luke did a wild cartwheel in front of me and slid on his stomach headfirst.

"NOOOOOO!" I screamed as a jagged rock — as big as me! — bounced over my head. Smaller rocks clattered past me as I fell.

I could see the other kids falling ... scrambling ... sliding down the mountain. Rocks banged and bumped and bounced close, just missing us.

A few seconds later, I landed in a heap at the bottom of the mountain. Rocks fell all around me. I ducked down and covered the back of my head with my hands.

The ground shook. I raised my head — in time to see a huge round rock roar down at me.

"OWWWW!" It hit the top of my head.

I waited for the crushing pain. Waited . . .

And started to laugh. "It's papier-mâché or something!" I shouted over the clattering and bumping of falling rocks. "It can't hurt us at all!"

Finally, the rock slide ended. We all climbed to our feet, shaking our heads. Some kids were laughing. I knew everyone was happy to be alive.

Matt and Robby started tossing fake rocks at each other. It became like a snowball battle with everyone joining in.

"What about Billy and Sheena?" Carly Beth shouted. "Everybody — stop! Did you forget Billy and Sheena?"

I raised my eyes to the cliff at the top. Billy and Sheena stood up there, leaning down, watching us.

"Wait. That's weird," I said. "Do they look farther away or what?"

Luke quickly agreed. "You're right, Lizzy. The mountain . . . it's TALLER!"

"They do look farther away," Julie said. "It's some kind of optical illusion, right?"

Matt cupped his hands around his mouth again and shouted to them. "Don't worry. We're coming!"

He led the way as we began to climb again.

The path was super slippery now. We kept slipping and sliding back.

"OW!" My feet slid out from under me again. I landed with a hard *thud* on my back. It knocked my breath out. I struggled to sit up.

And as I gazed to the top, Billy and Sheena looked even farther away!

"HELP!" Carly Beth let out a scream as she lost her balance and fell. She made a wild grab for Robby — and pulled him down with her.

We couldn't stop them. They rolled all the way down to the bottom.

"It's too slippery!" Jillian cried. "And look!" She pointed at the tiny figures of Billy and Sheena.

"The higher we climb, the farther away they are," Robby said.

"Is the mountain *growing*?" Julie asked, gazing straight up. "Or is it some kind of special effect?"

"It doesn't matter," I said. "We can't reach them by climbing. We'll never get up to the top."

"Lizzy is right," Matt said. "We need a better plan. Maybe — WHOOOOA!"

Before he could finish, he slipped. His feet shot out in front of him, and he hit the ground hard on his back.

Luke reached for him — too late. We all watched Matt slide down to the bottom, screaming the whole way. He landed headfirst next to Carly Beth and Robby.

The rest of us made our way down carefully.

Billy and Sheena were shouting to us from the mountaintop. But they were too far away. We couldn't make out their words. I turned and watched them wave their hands above their heads.

Did they think we were going to leave them there?

We huddled together, gazing up at them, trying to think of a way to get to them.

"Maybe some kind of vehicle," Robby said. "Some kind of four-wheel-drive Jeep or something."

Matt laughed. "Good luck finding one," he said.

"Well ... how did *they* get up there?" Carly Beth asked, pointing at Billy and Sheena.

Another flock of cawing crows flew over us. I felt a chill.

The sun was high in the sky, beaming down on the tall mountainside. But it cast no yellow light. Everything was a shade of gray — and the gray was actually making me DIZZY!

I'm in a different, frightening world, I thought. *A world with no color ... no warmth at all.*

And then Jackson spoke up, shaking me from my grim thoughts.

"I know what we can do," he said, glancing at his sister, Jillian.

"Of *course*!" Jillian cried. "Jackson, we should have thought of this before!"

13

Jackson raised his eyes to the two kids at the top of the mountain.

Wisps of gray fog floated overhead, making it hard to see them.

Jackson crossed his arms tightly over his chest. He narrowed his eyes and stared. He clenched his jaw as he concentrated.

Jillian must have seen the confused look on my face. She leaned toward me and whispered, "Jackson has powers. He can make things move."

Jackson moaned to himself. He gritted his teeth, concentrating hard.

And a few seconds later, Billy and Sheena came shooting down through the wisps of fog.

They were both screaming in shock. Their black hair blew above them as they dropped.

The fog appeared to part. Kicking their legs and thrashing their arms, the two kids came rocketing down toward us.

Faster . . . dropping faster . . .

Screaming the whole way.

I had this horrifying picture in my mind — the two of them crashing to the ground, splattering at our feet.

I sucked in a deep breath and held it. My heart thudded in my chest.

Billy and Sheena hovered above us for a few seconds. They came to a complete stop in the air. Sheena's hair fell over her face. Billy's long scream ended with a sharp intake of breath.

Jackson cried out, and his hands shot above his head. Then he waved the two kids down . . . waved them slowly down, as if they were on wires.

They landed gently on their feet.

Billy swallowed hard. His eyes were bulging. He was panting like a dog. He held on to his sister as if trying to stay on his feet.

Sheena took a shaky step toward us. She brushed back her hair and smiled. "Wow," she said. "That's the best ride yet!"

We all laughed. Some kids cheered. Matt slapped Jackson on the back. "Way to go, dude!"

We gathered happily around Billy and Sheena. We all shouted our questions at once.

"What happened? How did you get up there?"

"Where are the others? Are they okay?"

"Why were you on the mountain?"

Sheena raised a hand to silence us. She turned to Jackson. "How did you DO that?" she demanded. "How did you bring us down?"

Jackson grinned at her. "It's easy if you know how," he said.

Sheena turned to the rest of us. "I don't know where the other kids are," she said. "We lost them. We got separated."

"Sheena and I climbed the mountain to look for them," Billy said. "It was easy to climb up. But then . . ."

"We couldn't get down," Sheena said. She shuddered. "Billy and I have had a lot of creepy adventures in the past. But this park is *horrible!*"

"Those shadow people are everywhere," Billy said. "We didn't see anyone who is ALIVE!"

"And it's always gray and dark," Sheena added. "It's . . . it's scarier than HorrorLand." A sob escaped her throat. Her shoulders began to tremble.

Carly Beth wrapped her arms around Sheena. "You're okay now," she said softly. "We're all here with you."

"We're much safer here than in HorrorLand," Jillian said. "Byron told us that. We know we can trust Byron."

"We just have to find the other kids," Jackson said. "Then we can find a way to get home."

Carly Beth gave Sheena a tissue, and she wiped the tears from her eyes.

"I think we're in trouble," Billy said. "Sheena is the *brave* one in our family!"

Matt stepped up to Billy. "Have you seen Britney and Molly?"

"No," Billy answered.

"You escaped to Panic Park with your sister and four other kids," Matt said. "Michael, Sabrina, Boone, and Abby. How did you get separated from them?"

"I . . . I don't know," Billy replied.

"My dumb brother insisted we all go on this ride," Sheena said. "He got tired of waiting for the rest of you to come here."

"Don't call me dumb, stupid!" Billy snapped. "We didn't even know if the rest of you guys were coming or not," Billy said. "So we all went on a ride. It's called The Tunnel of Hate."

"The ride was open?" I asked. "Was someone running it?"

"I don't know," Billy answered. "It's a boat ride. Sheena and I got in the first boat. They came after us. It seemed like fun at first. But then . . . it got weird."

"Billy and I wanted to get out," Sheena said. "But when we turned around to look for the others . . . they were GONE!"

"They disappeared," Billy said. "They weren't in the tunnel. We searched for their boat. We couldn't find them."

"So we got out and looked for them," Sheena explained. "We wandered around the park. It's so totally creepy. And those frightening shadow people kept following us . . . watching us."

"We didn't know where to look," Billy said. "So we climbed the mountain. We thought we'd have a better view up there. But we didn't see them."

"Whoa. Wait a sec," Matt said. He locked his eyes on Billy. "You didn't see the other four kids anywhere else in the park. So do you think they might still be in The Tunnel of Hate?"

Billy and Sheena both shrugged.

"It's very dark in there," Sheena said. "Very hard to see anything."

"They *could* still be in there," Billy said.

Matt waved us forward. "Let's go for a boat ride," he said.

14

Two long canoes bobbed in the inky gray water in front of The Tunnel of Hate. The water lapped gently against the sides of the canoes as we climbed in.

Matt grabbed the paddle in the first canoe. Billy, Sheena, Carly Beth, and Julie dropped in with him.

Luke and I climbed into the back of the second canoe behind Jackson, Jillian, and Robby. The boat started to sink under our weight. Then it bobbed back up.

Jackson took the paddle. He dipped it into the water, testing it from side to side. "I'm pretty good at this," he said. "We went on a fifty-mile canoe trip at my camp last summer."

"Let's go. Keep close together," Matt called.

The canoes rolled slowly into the low tunnel. Staring into the blackness, I thought there was no light at all. But a few seconds later, my eyes adjusted. I could see the low tunnel roof and dim pinpoints of light in the water ahead of us.

We sat in silence, staring straight ahead. The only sound was the steady *splash splash splash* of the paddles as Matt and Jackson pulled us deeper into the tunnel.

The narrow waterway ran straight, no bends or curves. The dark water was gentle and flat, lapping softly at our sides.

What a boring ride, I thought.

"I don't see anyone else in here," Carly Beth murmured. "The tunnel is empty."

"This is a waste of time," Robby said.

"Give it a chance," Matt said, paddling hard. "We don't know how long this tunnel is. The others could still be lost in here."

"That's stupid," Robby snapped.

Matt stopped paddling. "Who are you calling stupid?" he shouted.

The canoes bobbed side by side.

"Don't start arguing," Jillian said.

"Shut up!" Matt screamed at her.

"YOU shut up!" Jillian cried. "What's your problem, Fat Face?"

"Don't call us names, Dirt Breath!" Robby shouted at Jillian.

Suddenly, Billy took a swing at Matt. Matt ducked, and Billy nearly toppled over the side of the canoe.

"Stupid jerk!"

"You want a piece of me?" Matt screamed. He punched Billy hard in the chest. Billy groaned and slumped to the canoe seat.

Everyone started screaming at once.

Luke turned to me angrily and shook his fist. "This is all your fault, Lizzy. I never wanted to come here."

"My fault?" I cried. "You little mouse-faced wimp!"

Luke grabbed at me. The canoe rocked hard to one side.

"Stop it! *Stop* it!" Carly Beth screamed. She turned to Julie. "Stop shoving me, you big baby."

"I'M a baby?!" Julie shrieked. "You idiot! YOU'RE a big baby — and a scaredy-cat. You think you're so cute because you look like a little elf. But you're a total CREEP!"

"Jerk!" Carly Beth screamed at Julie. "Big Butt Face!" She gave Julie a hard shove with her elbow.

"Stop it!" I screamed. "Stop it, you morons!"

"I HATE you!" Luke shrieked at me. He began pounding his fists against my back. "I HATE you! I HATE you!"

"Luke, you're the biggest jerk here!" I shot back.

"Shut up! Shut up! Shut up!" he screamed.

"YOU shut up! YOU shut up!" I screamed back at him.

I couldn't help myself. I knew what was happening. The Tunnel of Hate was for *real*. It made people hate each other.

I could see it happening. But I couldn't stop it. And I could feel myself hating everyone, even my brother, Luke.

In the other canoe, Julie grabbed Carly Beth's hair and gave it a hard pull.

Carly Beth uttered a cry of pain. Then she wrapped her hands around Julie's throat and tried to choke her.

Julie slapped Carly Beth's hands away. Then she let out a long, shrill animal wail — *"AAAAIIIIIEEEEE!"* She dove at Carly Beth, tackling her around the waist.

Their canoe tipped to the side.

Grunting and sobbing, Carly Beth and Julie wrestled.

"Stop it, you stupid idiots! STOP!" I screamed.

"Shut your ugly FACE!" Robby shouted at me.

And then I gasped as Carly Beth and Julie went tumbling out of their canoe.

They hit the water with a loud splash. It sent a tall wave rolling over the canoe as the two girls plunged out of sight.

"Good riddance!" Robby cried.

"I hate you!" Jillian screeched at Robby. "Why don't you jump in with them?"

"Why don't YOU?" Robby shot back. He swiped the paddle from Jackson's hands and swung it at Jillian's head.

Missed.

I grabbed the side of the canoe and leaned over the edge. I peered down into the dark water. Waiting for Julie and Carly Beth to come splashing up to the surface.

Waiting . . .

The water so flat. So still.

As if no one were down there.

I squeezed the side of the canoe so hard, my hands ached. I stared down without blinking. Without breathing.

My heart started to pound. I cupped my hands around my mouth and shouted: "Carly Beth? Julie? You stupid jerks!"

Where were they? Where *were* they?

No splashing. No air bubbles. Nothing at all.

I let out a shuddering sob. The two girls weren't coming back up.

I yelled to Matt. "Listen to me, moron! Someone has to jump in!" I cried. "Someone —"

Matt had his hands wrapped around Billy's throat. Billy swung both fists, pounding Matt's chest.

Then the two canoes crashed into each other.

Still no sign of Julie and Carly Beth.

"Stop it, you dumb geeks! Stop it!" I screamed to the two boys.

"Put a sock in it!" Jackson snapped at me. "Shut your stupid yap!"

"But . . . but . . . they're DROWNING!" I cried.

I turned to my brother. He stared back at me, his face filled with hate. "You stink out loud," he muttered.

I ignored his anger. "We have to jump in, Creep Face," I said. "We have to find those girls. Maybe it will prove to those other idiots that we're on their side."

"Go take a hike," Luke replied. He stuck his tongue out and spit at me.

A wave of anger swept over me. I wanted to punch the little punk's teeth down his throat.

Instead, I grabbed his hand — tugged — and pulled him over the side of the canoe with me.

"HEEEEEY!" He let out a fierce scream.

We both hit the water at the same time.

I shuddered, startled by how cold it was. Water seeped into my mouth, and I started to choke.

Luke slapped my hand away and began thrashing his arms furiously, struggling to pull himself back up to the surface.

But I turned and dove down, squinting into the dark waters.

Where were they?

The canal was narrow. Not much room to swim. But deeper than I'd thought.

It didn't take long to find Carly Beth and Julie. They were down at the bottom. Still wrestling. Still punching each other and pulling hair and wrestling.

They hate each other so much, they don't care if they DROWN, I told myself.

My chest started to ache. I couldn't hold my breath much longer.

I turned and saw Luke at my side. He kept fading in and out, ghostly in the dark water.

I motioned to him, and he followed. He grabbed Julie by the shoulders and tried to pull her away.

I wrapped my hands around Carly Beth's waist. And pulled.

The girls tried to shove Luke and me away. They were furious that we were trying to break up their battle.

But I wouldn't let go. My chest felt about to burst. Every muscle ached.

I pulled Carly Beth away from Julie — and rose up . . . up to the surface.

We both burst over the water, sputtering and choking. I gasped in breath after breath.

I gave Carly Beth a big push. She slumped limply into our canoe. She didn't have any fight left in her.

Brushing my wet hair from my eyes, I turned and helped my brother shove Julie into the other canoe. Then I grabbed his hands and tugged him into our canoe.

I was drenched. Cold and shivering. My wet clothes clung to my body. I couldn't catch my breath.

I glanced up to see Matt in his canoe holding the paddle above his head. "Toss the girls back in!" he shouted to me. "Go ahead! If they want to swim, throw them back in. DO it!"

"Matt — please," I begged. "Sit down."

"Shut up!" Robby snapped. "Don't tell Matt what to do."

"Yeah. Who do you think you are? A big hero?" Jillian sneered. She moved toward me. "Want to go for another swim, Lizzy?"

"Stop it, you dumb clucks! Everyone just go die!" I cried.

"You want a piece of me?" Matt cried again. "You're going down, Lizzy."

"You whiny baby!" Jillian screamed. "You total loser!"

"Don't you morons see what has happened?" I cried. "The Tunnel of Hate is making us *hate* each other. We have to get out of here — as fast as we can."

Carly Beth was still slumped against the side of our canoe. She groaned. Her eyes were half shut and her arms hung lifelessly at her sides.

In the other canoe, Julie stared straight ahead, dazed. She hadn't even brushed the matted tangles of wet hair off her face.

"Do you see? Do you see what the tunnel has done to us?" I repeated.

"We can see, you stupid idiot!" Robby shouted.

The canoes drifted side by side, moving slowly through the tunnel. Eerie gray lights darted under the surface of the water, like glowing minnows.

I couldn't stop shivering. Didn't this ride ever *end*?

Everyone was shouting angrily. Matt and Jackson were going at each other with the canoe paddles. Matt toppled backward and nearly fell into our canoe.

Suddenly, everyone stopped. And stared in shocked silence up ahead.

"It's another canoe!" I whispered.

I squinted into the inky light. A long canoe was wedged against the side of the tunnel.

"Hey! There they are!" Carly Beth cried.

Yes. As we drifted closer, I saw four kids turn their faces to us.

I recognized them from my research. Sabrina, Michael, Boone, and Abby.

And then I spotted two girls slumped in the front of the canoe. Molly and Britney!

We all started to cheer.

Matt and Billy waved wildly to the other boat.

"Hey — are you okay?"

"Dudes, what are you doing there?"

"Are you stuck?"

"We've been searching everywhere for you, you stupid idiots!"

The kids in the boat didn't move. They didn't cheer or wave back.

Finally, Britney raised her face to us — and growled like an animal.

Molly grunted and swiped her hands at us, like she was trying to claw us.

I could see thick drool running down Boone's chin. He growled like an angry dog — and snapped his jaws again and again.

"Loooook out! He bites!" Molly screeched — and started to howl.

The others grunted and barked and snapped their jaws. They tore at their hair and acted like deranged zoo animals. Yellow snot ran out of their noses.

"They . . . they've been in the tunnel a long time," Billy muttered. "*Too* long. We should leave them behind!"

A shiver ran down my back. As we drifted closer to them, I stared in horror at the growling, snarling kids. "They've turned into animals," I murmured. "Wild beasts. Disgusting!"

"What are we going to do with these losers?" Matt asked. "What CAN we do?"

16

Our canoes drifted closer to them.

Boone stood up in the long boat and pounded his chest like a gorilla. He was big and strong looking. His eyes were wild and his face turned red with rage. He let out a roar and pounded his chest some more.

Michael stood up and joined him, thumping his chest and grunting like a gorilla.

Sabrina tossed back her head and screamed, a shrill hyena scream. Then she clawed her hands at us.

Carly Beth gasped. "Sabrina? It's me. You idiot — I'm your best friend — remember?"

Sabrina glared at Carly Beth. Then she lowered her head and vomited something green into the water.

"Ohhhh, this is HORRIBLE!" Carly Beth moaned. "We've been friends since kindergarten! And look at her. Look at her now! She's a loser."

Sabrina giggled and vomited again.

"Watch out!" I screamed.

I saw Michael pull his arm back — and *heave* the paddle at us.

"OWWW!" Matt cried out, and grabbed his shoulder as the paddle smacked him hard and splashed into the water.

The kids on the other boat all hooted and bounced up and down. They clawed their hands at us and snapped their jaws.

"We have to get them out of the tunnel," I said.

"But how, you moron?" Carly Beth asked. "They really want to hurt us."

"They're . . . they're dangerous," Luke stammered. "And you're stupid."

"How can we fight them?" Robby murmured. "They're ANIMALS."

Our canoes floated closer. In a few seconds, the boats would touch.

A shrill scream echoed through the narrow tunnel. I watched in horror as Britney sank her teeth into Molly's throat. Grunting and snapping at each other like wolves, the two girls wrestled.

"Stop it! STOP it!" Carly Beth screamed.

Matt's canoe bumped the back of their boat.

With a terrifying roar, Michael reached into the canoe and grabbed Matt around the waist,

66

lifted him into the air, and tried to toss him into the water.

Then my canoe bumped into the back of Matt's canoe — and both boys toppled to their knees.

"Stop! Stop it, you jerks!" I cried. "We'll DROWN in here! We —"

I choked on my words as Sabrina wrapped her hands around my throat. Her eyes bulged. Her mouth was open in a high animal cry of fury. She started to squeeze.

Tighter . . .

I couldn't breathe. I slapped at her hands.

Couldn't move her. Couldn't breathe . . .

And then everything froze.

Was I *dying*?

No. I slid out from Sabrina's grasp. She didn't move. Her hands stayed curled in the air.

Gasping for breath, I saw that everyone in Boone's boat had frozen in place. No one moved. No one blinked.

"Huh?" My heart still pounding, I turned and saw Jackson staring hard at the frozen kids.

His eyes were locked in a steady gaze. His jaw was clenched. He concentrated hard.

"Stop staring at me, you loser. I'm using my powers to hold them still," he said. "Quick — pull their canoe away from the side. We'll push them out of the tunnel."

That's just what we did.

Matt and Sheena leaned over the side and tugged Boone's canoe free. Then we paddled hard, pushing their boat ahead of us.

Jackson kept his gaze on the frozen kids, concentrating his powers on them. I could see that it was a struggle. Sweat poured down his forehead. He gritted his teeth so hard, his cheeks turned bright red.

It seemed to take days. The tunnel stretched straight ahead, black except for the tiny darting lights in the water.

No one spoke. The only sound was the splash of the paddles and the gentle lap of the water against the sides of the canoes.

Finally, I saw a circle of gray light up ahead. The tunnel exit.

Dark trees came into view. A couple of buildings. Our three canoes bobbed out into the light.

Jackson got us to a wooden dock. I jumped to my feet. I couldn't wait to get on land!

Jackson finally shut his eyes. He let out a long sigh. The frozen kids began to move, stretching their arms, their necks.

Boone squinted at us. I could see the confusion on his face. "What . . . what happened back there?" he asked.

"Where did you guys come from?" Abby demanded, brushing her hair into place with her hands. "I didn't see you. How did you find us?"

They didn't seem to remember what the tunnel had done to them.

I knew I'd never forget it.

I took some long, deep breaths. I could feel the hate sliding off me, fading away.

"Sabrina, I'm so glad you're okay," Carly Beth said. She rushed forward to hug Sabrina. "Do you feel . . . normal now?"

Sabrina nodded. "I . . . I guess."

We all scrambled onto the shore. I gazed around.

We were standing on the edge of a large grassy circle. On the other side of the circle stood rides and other attractions. All dark. All empty.

Behind the rides, a tall building rose up. It looked like a castle. Wisps of fog swam in front of its twin towers. The black roof slanted sharply down with small round windows along the top.

Carly Beth and Julie stepped up to Luke and me. "Thank you," Carly Beth said. "You know. For jumping in after us."

"Thank you for saving our lives," Julie said. "It was crazy in there. We . . . we just lost it."

"Maybe we were wrong about you two," Carly Beth said.

That made me feel good. But behind them, I saw Jillian glaring at me suspiciously.

"I'm just glad we made it out of that tunnel," I said.

"But *now* what?" Luke demanded.

Everyone started talking at once. I took a step back and counted. There were sixteen of us now. Sixteen kids who had traveled here from HorrorLand.

Were we the only living people in Panic Park?

Britney and Molly hung back, away from the others. They talked quietly to each other. They both seemed dazed. They kept blinking against the harsh gray light.

Billy and Sheena turned to them. "You two have been in Panic Park the longest," Billy said. "Tell us what you've seen."

Kids began peppering Britney and Molly with questions.

"What have you been doing here?"

"Did you try to get back to HorrorLand?"

"Have you seen anyone else?"

"Did you find an exit?"

The two girls clung together. They kept blinking and shaking their heads.

"I . . . don't remember much," Molly said. "It's like . . ."

"It's like being in a fog or something," Britney said.

"I remember going through a mirror in a café," Molly said. "And we were here in Panic Park. And we were on a ride."

"Yes. A carousel," Britney said. "It had flames coming out the sides. But it didn't burn. And . . .

and . . . I remember going back to Horror-Land once."

"Yes. We went back," Molly agreed. "We saw Robby. Playing a game in the arcade."

"How?" Robby demanded. "How did you get back there?"

"Tell us!" Matt stepped up beside Robby. "Tell us how you got back to HorrorLand. We need to know. We need to get out of Panic Park."

The girls stared blankly at us.

"I don't remember," Britney said. Her chin trembled. "I feel so weird. Like my brain is in a cloud or something."

Molly shook her head. "I don't remember, either. I feel like I'm sleepwalking. Or not really awake."

Then I saw the park guide. Matt had folded it up and stuffed it into the back pocket of his jeans.

"Matt — the guide," I said, pointing. "It will show us an exit."

He pulled the booklet from his pocket and opened it. The park map fell out with it.

I picked it up and started to unfold it. But I stopped when I saw a flash of color.

Green and purple, moving toward us through the black-and-white park.

It took me a few seconds to realize I was staring at a HorrorLand Horror.

"Byron!" Carly Beth shouted as the big creature came running full speed across the pavement.

His big chest was heaving under the bib of his green overalls. He was breathing noisily. "Thank goodness I've found you!" he cried in his booming, deep voice.

But Carly Beth turned on him angrily. "You *tricked* us!" she shouted.

The others were angry, too.

"This park is terrifying!"

"How could you send us here?"

"It's more dangerous than HorrorLand!"

"We were nearly KILLED!" Julie cried.

Byron raised both furry paws as if surrendering. "I know. I know," he said. "I'm so sorry."

"But *you're* the one who told us we'd be safer here," Matt said. "You're the one who helped us get here."

"They tricked me, too," Byron replied. "They *used* me! They lied to me."

We all stared at him. Was he telling the truth?

"I'll get you out of this place — now," Byron said, glancing around. "The park is dead. It's no place for living creatures."

"We trusted you before," Matt said. "How do we know we can trust you now?"

"I'll get you to a safe place. Promise," Byron

said. "But we have to hurry. Come on —
follow me."

No one moved.

"How do we know if we can trust him?" Michael
asked Matt. "He tricked us before. Maybe he's
tricking us now."

"No. Listen to me —" Byron said.

Matt turned to Jillian. "You can read minds,
right?"

Jillian nodded.

"Well, read Byron's mind," Matt said. "Tell
us — is he lying? Is this another trick?"

Jillian narrowed her eyes at Byron.

We huddled together in silence, watching . . .
waiting.

"Yes," Jillian said finally. "I'm reading his
thoughts. . . ."

17

Byron frowned at Jillian. "This is crazy. You're wasting time."

"Is he telling the truth?" Matt asked her.

Jillian nodded. "Yes. It's not a trick. He wants to help us."

"Whew. That's good news," Matt said. He gave Byron a high five. "Tell us what to do."

"Follow me," Byron said. "There's only one way out of here."

He started walking toward the rides, swinging his big furry arms, taking long strides. We had to jog to keep up with him.

We passed three shadow people, nearly hidden in the shade of an empty shop. Their heads turned to follow us as we hurried by. But they didn't move.

Luke hurried up beside me. "I don't think we can trust this Horror," I whispered.

"But Jillian read his mind," Luke said.

"Yes," I whispered. "But Jillian said she read MY mind — and she was wrong."

"Her brother's powers are real," Luke said. He frowned. "I don't know *what* to think."

Byron turned suddenly and began to follow a curving path into a thick grove of trees.

"What should we do?" Luke whispered.

"We have to stick with the other kids," I replied. "Maybe Byron will get us back to HorrorLand, where it's safe."

"Maybe . . ." Luke said quietly.

Crows cawed in the trees overhead. I saw another shadow person watching us as we passed. I turned to stare at him, and he ducked behind a broad tree trunk.

Byron stopped in front of two tall hedges. The hedges stretched way over our heads, all pine needles and prickly thorns. I peered into the narrow opening between the two hedges. Dark inside. Darker than night.

"Be careful. Those thorns are sharp," Byron warned.

"Where are we?" Carly Beth asked.

"The entrance to The Midnight Maze," Byron replied. He glanced around nervously. "It's a maze where time stands still. It's always midnight inside the maze."

Michael leaned into the narrow space between

the hedges. "Are we supposed to go in there?" he asked.

Byron nodded. "The maze leads out of Panic Park," he said. "It will take you back to our world. It's the only exit."

"Huh?" Michael kept staring into the black space. "Are you joking? This is the only way out of Panic Park? Where's the front gate?"

"There is no front gate," Byron answered. "Check out the map. You'll see. This is the only exit."

I felt my throat tighten in fear. I don't like narrow, dark places.

Last Halloween, Mom and Dad took us to a haunted house that had been set up downtown. You know. The kind where you pay admission. Then you walk through creepy, dark halls and people in costumes leap out at you and try to make you scream.

I hated it. It really frightened me.

I'm usually pretty brave. But I just couldn't stand being closed up in those twisting, dark halls.

And now, staring into the black opening between the hedges brought that fear back.

"Is . . . is it a hard maze?" I stammered.

Byron nodded. He rubbed the curled horns that poked out from the top of his head. "Stick together, and you should be okay," he said softly.

"How long does it take?" I asked.

"Depends," Byron replied. "Just stay close. Don't get separated. I see the looks on your faces. I know you're scared. And it's a scary maze. But if you can find your way out, you'll be safe. I promise."

"Whoa. Wait a minute," Boone said. "Does that mean you're not coming with us?"

Byron glanced around again. "I'm going to stay here and guard the entrance," he said in a whisper. "I'll make sure no one follows you."

"Who would follow us?" I asked. "We haven't seen *anyone* in this park. Who wants to harm us? Who?"

"No time now," Byron replied.

He gave me a gentle push into the entrance of the maze. "Go, go, go," he said. "Hurry."

I stepped between the hedges. The others followed.

The air felt heavy and cold inside the maze. I could smell something stale and sour. Like when something has been left too long in the fridge.

The hedges formed tall walls on both sides of us. We began to follow them down a long, straight passageway. Matt took the lead.

Behind us, I heard Byron at the maze entrance. "Good luck!" he called.

18

We walked slowly, following the hedge walls. Tall, leafy trees overhead blocked the light from the sky, making it as dark as midnight.

The passage was so narrow, we had to walk in single file. "Watch out. It turns here," Matt called from the front of the line.

The ground beneath us was soft and damp. My sneakers sank into the dirt. I had to keep raising my knees to pull them out.

I was nearly at the end of the line, right behind Luke. I walked carefully and kept my shoulders hunched. The long, pointed thorns poking out of the hedge walls looked very sharp.

"Careful. It slants down," Matt called. His voice sounded far away, muffled by the thick hedge walls.

"How long *is* this thing?" Robby called.

We made another sharp turn.

"Are we walking in circles?" Sheena asked from behind me.

My heart was pounding, making a fluttery feeling in my chest. I wiped sweat off my forehead with the sleeve of my top.

We turned again. The darkness seemed to deepen. I could barely see Luke in front of me.

We found ourselves in a large square area. Nothing there. Just empty space.

"How do we know we went the right way?" Boone asked.

"We don't know," Carly Beth said. "It's a maze — right? We just have to keep exploring till we find the way out."

"But it's totally dark," Sabrina said. "We could wander around in here forever!"

"Just keep walking," Matt said. "We're okay so far, aren't we?"

We followed the hedges to another square area. My sneaker stuck in the mud. I tried to pull it out, but it wouldn't budge.

"Hey!" I let out a cry as both of my shoes started to sink.

"It's muddy here!" Michael called.

"I . . . I think I'm stuck!" Robby said.

"Oh, yuck! The mud is way soft!" Abby cried.

I bent down to pull one sneaker free — and gasped. The mud seeped over my ankles. I was sinking fast!

"It . . . it's like quicksand!" Abby cried. "Oh, help!"

I felt the mud rise up on my legs, thick and wet. It felt so COLD! I slapped at the mud, and it stuck to my hands like cold pudding.

My knees were covered. I couldn't move my legs. Through my jeans, I felt the cold mud wrap around my thighs.

Kids began to scream and cry out for help.

Ahead of me, I saw Billy reach for the hedge to help pull himself out. But he screamed and jerked his hands back as thorns cut into his skin.

"We're going to DROWN in this mud!" Michael cried.

"Don't move!" Carly Beth shouted. "The more you move, the faster you sink!"

"We HAVE to move!" Julie cried. "If we don't move, we'll just go under SLOWER!"

"It's like it's ALIVE!" Billy screamed. "The mud . . . it's pulling me. I can feel it pulling me down!"

Fear choked my throat. I sucked in a shuddering breath. The cold mud was sliding over me. Soon it would be packed around my waist.

I slapped at it again. Tried to push myself up. But my hands sank into the thick, cold goo.

Kids were screaming and struggling.

"Help! Somebody — help pull me up!"

"It's so thick! Like cement!"

"Grab on to me. Maybe if we both pull . . ."

I forced myself to breathe. I hugged myself, trying to stop my body from shivering. Trying to hug away my fear.

"Luke!" I called to my brother. I reached out for him. But he was too far away.

The mud had reached his waist. He held his hands high above his head. He was twisting and squirming, trying to force his way up from the muck.

And then . . . *BUMP*.

My shoes bumped into something hard.

I froze and held my breath.

What just happened?

A hush fell over us. I glanced around. Everyone had stopped squirming and struggling.

"Hey — I stopped sinking!" I shouted.

I leaned forward, then back. I raised my right foot a little, then set it back down.

"I . . . I hit bottom!" I cried.

"Me, too!" Matt exclaimed. "It's hard underneath. We're not going to sink over our heads!"

We all began to rock back and forth, leaning one way, then the other. It created holes in the mud, large enough for us to pull ourselves up.

Michael struggled out first. Then he went around tugging other kids free.

We hurried from the muddy square, following the hedge walls around a sharp curve.

"I'm covered in mud," Julie wailed. "I'll never get these jeans clean. I'll just have to throw them away. And . . . and look at my sneakers!"

"My jeans are getting *stiff*," Sabrina said. "The mud is caked on! And it STINKS!"

"Who cares about a little mud?" Matt said. "If it gets us out of Panic Park."

"Watch out for other traps," Robby said. "This maze is probably packed with nasty surprises."

We turned another corner — then stopped.

The overhead trees gave way. And a bright gray light poured down on us.

I blinked, trying to adjust to the startling light. And stared at a line of six giant eggs. Six eggs standing on end, almost as big as cars.

I heard a cracking sound. I held my breath and listened hard. Another long *craaaaack*.

I saw a jagged split in the egg on one end of the line. And then more cracks along the speckled white shells of the other huge eggs.

The eggs were HATCHING.

"Is this for *real*?" Carly Beth cried. "Are they DINOSAUR eggs?"

"They've got to be fakes," Robby said.

Michael stepped in front of us. "No! Stand back!" He waved his big arms in front of him, motioning us back.

Another loud cracking sound. A ragged chunk of eggshell fell to the ground at Michael's feet.

"I recognize these eggs," Michael said.

Craaaaaack craaack.

"These are monster eggs. There are monsters in there. I had to fight them. Back home. I had to BECOME one!"

"How totally weird," I muttered.

I couldn't take my eyes off the cracking shells.

The eggs were taller than me. And the way they glowed in the eerie, gray light... The way they glowed...

... drew me closer.

I couldn't help myself. They were so ... interesting.

Without realizing it, I stepped up to one of the eggs.

A loud *craaaack* made me gasp.

And a goo-covered green hand shot out — and twisted its claws around my throat.

19

I opened my mouth in a shrill scream.

The tough claws tightened around my neck and cut off the scream.

The egg cracked open. Jagged shards of shell dropped to the ground. Yellowish goo poured out from the bottom.

A green lizardlike creature staggered out. Its black tongue lashed at the layer of mucus on its warty face.

I ducked and twisted my body, trying to free myself from its grip.

Newly hatched, its claws were slimy and wet. I slid free and dove toward the other kids.

They were screaming and gaping in horror as the other giant eggs cracked open. Five more skinny green monsters came pouring out with the disgusting yolky liquid.

They tore at the thick mucus that covered their faces and bodies. They rolled their bulging black eyes and snapped their jaws. One of them blew a big bubble of mucus that popped — and sprayed over me.

"Ohhhh, gross!" I let out a moan and staggered back.

The monsters took their first steps, lurching forward. Broken eggshells crunched under their large lizard feet. They worked their front legs, stretching and reaching, testing them.

Their dark eyes locked on us. They began to circle us. They raised pointed claws, still wet and sticky. Low growls rumbled from deep in their bellies.

"This isn't fake," Carly Beth muttered. "They're REAL!"

"Like I said, I . . . I know them," Michael said. "I had to fight monsters just like these back home."

He picked up a big chunk of eggshell and heaved it at one of the ugly creatures. It hit the monster's chest and bounced off.

The monster opened its jaws in an angry roar — and snapped at Michael.

Michael dropped to his knees beside me.

"Are you okay?" I cried. I reached down to help him back up.

Michael pushed my hands away. "No," he said. "I know what I have to do."

The monsters circled us faster, swiping their claws in the air.

"Michael — get up!" I cried. "They're going to attack!"

"I have to deal with it," he said. "Watch out, guys. One more monster on the way!"

He crawled over broken pieces of shell to the bottom piece of an egg, dripping with yellow yolk.

"Michael — NO!" Carly Beth cried.

"What are you DOING?" Abby screamed.

Michael lowered his face into the yolk and began to drink.

20

The monsters stopped circling. They grew silent as they watched.

Michael buried his face in the jagged shell bottom. He slurped the thick yellow goo noisily.

My stomach heaved. What was he *doing*? How could he drink that disgusting sticky yolk?

We all watched in horror as Michael finally raised his head. He turned to us. The thick yolk covered his cheeks and ran down his chin.

He swallowed. Once. Twice.

Slowly, he climbed to his feet.

"Michael?" Carly Beth called.

He stared past her at the monsters. For a few seconds, nothing happened. No one moved.

Then I saw Michael begin to change.

His eyes bulged. His face lengthened. His nose stretched ... stretched over his mouth ... and formed an animal snout.

Two rows of jagged teeth slid out from black lips. Michael's skin darkened . . . darkened to an olive-green color.

His body grew. The arms lengthened. His chest spread wide . . . wider . . . until his T-shirt ripped open.

Claws curled out from his long fingers. He tossed back his monstrous head and let out a deafening roar.

It took only seconds for him to become one of them.

And then he roared forward. Dove at the startled creatures. Swiping his claws wildly ahead of him.

I grabbed Luke and we staggered back. The other kids stumbled out of the way.

I wanted to run. I wanted to hide.

I didn't want to watch the horrifying fight. But I couldn't take my eyes off Michael as he attacked the six newborn creatures.

He dug his fangs into a throat. Swiped his sharp claws down the monster's chest.

The monster bleated like a lamb as rivers of black blood leaked down its front. With a long groan, the monster fell, defeated.

Michael roared on to the next. Bellowing like a movie dinosaur, he raked his claws over its face, then dug his jagged teeth into its throat.

He swiped at the startled monsters, ripping their still-sticky skin apart, head butting, punching, kicking, tearing their bodies with his powerful fangs.

Frozen in fear, I held on to Luke, and we watched the deadly battle. In less than a minute, all six monsters lay sprawled on the ground. Not moving. Their eyes staring up, blank and lifeless.

Michael raised his face to the sky and roared. A victory roar.

He pounded his bulging green chest with both fists. He roared and stomped his huge feet. Stomped and danced and roared some more.

He . . . he's out of control! I thought. *He's really a MONSTER!*

Then, with an animal grunt, he spun away from the dead monsters. He stepped over one. It made a wet *squissssh* as his foot sank into its belly.

Michael stepped off it and stomped toward me, smashing his jaws together.

Out of control . . . Out of control!

He locked his eyes on me — and growled angrily. He raised his claws to attack.

And leaped at me!

21

"NOOOOOO!"

I uttered a terrified shriek — and dodged to my right.

I lurched so hard, I fell. And landed on my side.

I heard the other kids screaming.

Gasping in horror, I spun around.

It took me a few seconds to realize that Michael *wasn't* attacking me.

He leaped past me to the broken egg. Dropped to his knees. Lowered his head and once again began noisily lapping up the yolk.

It sounded like a dog at its water dish.

He groaned as he sucked down the thick, sticky goo.

When he finally raised his head, he was Michael again. Blinking, he rubbed goo from his eyes. He climbed to his feet and wiped his chin with his torn T-shirt.

He let out a long sigh. "Sorry about that," he said. He grabbed my arms and helped pull me to my feet. His hands were sticky from the egg yolk.

"That . . . happened to you before?" I asked.

He nodded. "I'm still part monster. Can't seem to get rid of it."

Matt pointed to the dead monsters at our feet. "Maybe being part monster is a GOOD thing," he said.

Our shoes crunched over the broken pieces of eggshell as we started to walk. Matt and Michael led the way, following the tall hedge walls.

The charcoal-colored sky above our heads provided the only light. A flock of shadowy birds, cawing loudly, soared over our heads.

"Probably more crows," Luke muttered.

He turned to me. And even in the dim light, I could see the fear on my little brother's face.

"Lizzy, how do we know we're going the right way? How do we know this maze leads out of Panic Park?"

The same questions were frightening me. I didn't know how to answer him.

The ground grew hard. A cold wind blew over us.

We came to another split in the hedges. Two paths, each leading in a different direction. I could see only darkness down both paths.

"Which one?" Matt asked, scratching his head.

"Maybe we should split up," Boone said. "Some of us go this way, some go the other."

"No way," Jackson said. "Did you forget what Byron told us? He said to stick together — no matter what."

"Jackson is right," Carly Beth said. "We all want to get out of this place together. Let's try the path on the left. If it doesn't lead anywhere, we can turn around and come back. Then take the path to the right."

The cawing birds flew overhead again, this time in the other direction. Their cries were raspy and hoarse. Were they trying to warn us about something?

The sound sent a shiver down my back.

We started walking again, two by two, following the path to the left. My side ached from where I'd fallen on it. The mud caked on my jeans smelled like sour milk.

Luke and I walked near the front of the line, behind Matt and Michael. Michael kept muttering about the monsters. "How did they get to Panic Park?" he wondered. "I defeated them all back home. So how could they follow me here?"

Matt opened his mouth to answer, but he didn't get a word out.

A girl screamed behind us. I turned and saw that it was Carly Beth.

She pointed straight ahead. And screamed again. "No! NO! I don't *believe* it!"

I squinted hard into the dim light. And the masks slowly came into focus.

A line of ugly masks . . . monstrous-looking human faces floating in the air.

At first I thought they were dangling from a rope or wire. But as we took a few steps closer, I saw that they were floating free. Rising and falling like saggy helium balloons.

"Oh, noooo!" Carly Beth wailed. "Don't you see? These things — these horrible THINGS are all following us! First HorrorLand — now here!"

We stopped a few feet from the masks and gazed up at them.

Their deep, empty eyeholes appeared to stare down at us. Their fat, rubbery lips bobbed up and down.

The faces were hideous — warty and fang toothed, stringy hair standing straight up, the cheeks puffy and fat . . . red sores on the foreheads . . . cuts and wounds and stitch marks.

"Halloween masks?" Julie asked quietly.

"No. They're *alive*," Carly Beth said.

And as she said it, the masks began to speak.

They made jabbering sounds in deep, rumbling voices, so low I couldn't make out the words.

The rubbery lips bounced up and down. The empty eyes gazed blankly down at us. Their eerie voices were a rumble of grunts and groans.

Matt took a flying leap and tried to grab one and pull it down.

But it shot up out of his reach.

That seemed to make the masks angry. They began jabbering louder, their lips bobbing faster, cheeks puffing in and out.

"You can't help me," Carly Beth said, her voice trembling. "I have to deal with them."

Her friend Sabrina pulled her back. "Carly Beth — no!"

"They've come for me," Carly Beth said. She shrugged Sabrina away. "They've come for me."

She stepped forward until she was right under the ugly, mumbling faces.

"You've come for *me* — right?" she shouted up to them.

An evil-looking green mask floated lower. Its mouth hung open, revealing two rows of vicious, curled fangs. The cheeks and forehead were cracked and rutted. Its eyeholes were ringed with dark red blood.

"The Haunted Mask! You've come for me," Carly Beth repeated, saying it almost like a chant. "You've come for me. . . ."

"Carly Beth — DON'T!" Sabrina screamed.

Too late.

"You've come for me. . . . You've come for me!"

Carly Beth grabbed the ugly mask from the air — and pulled it down over her head.

22

"Carly Beth — NO! Take it off!" Sabrina screamed.

She dove at Carly Beth and grabbed for the mask.

But Carly Beth twisted out of Sabrina's reach.

"It's tightening against her face!" Sabrina yelled. "It's already tightening!"

Yes. I could see the green mask stretching over Carly Beth's cheeks, tightening under her chin.

We all stood and watched in horror. We didn't know what to do.

We knew this was a foe Carly Beth and Sabrina had faced back home. But we had no idea what would happen next.

The ugly mask appeared to melt against Carly Beth's face . . . melt right into her skin.

And then the disgusting mouth hole with its curled teeth dropped open. And Carly Beth let out a roar ... an animal roar ... not a human sound. A cry of pure evil.

The booming roar sent a chill to the back of my neck. My muscles all tensed.

Carly Beth raised her masked face to the sky and roared again.

I pressed my hands over my ears. I knew the horrifying cry didn't come from Carly Beth. It came from something evil ... something screaming out its rage.

The other ugly masks froze in midair.

The Haunted Mask was Carly Beth's face now. It had wrapped itself around her until it *became* her. The rubbery, fanged mouth was *her* mouth. Her eyes peered out at us angrily through the rings of dark, caked blood.

With another frightening roar, Carly Beth leaped high — and grabbed one of the masks out of the air. She held it in front of her with both hands — and RIPPED it in half.

"AAAAAAIIII!" The mask let out a high, shrill scream of pain.

Carly Beth dropped the mask to the ground. I gasped. I could hear the two halves making little cries.

Carly Beth stamped on it until it stopped whimpering. Then she leaped again and brought down another mask.

Grunting like a hungry animal, she ripped the mask to pieces.

The mask groaned and cried. Then it went silent as it hit the ground.

Two more masks floated above us in the gray sky. They made no attempt to escape. It was like they were waiting their turn.

They squealed and cried as Carly Beth ripped them apart. She stamped on the rubbery pieces.

Then she turned to us, raised both hands as if ready to attack, and let out a bleating sound, an animal cry of pain.

"You're NEXT!" she screamed in a hoarse, deep voice — the voice of the evil mask. "You're NEXT! Do you think you can just stand there? Do you think you can ESCAPE my RAGE?"

Without warning, she leaped at the nearest person — her friend Sabrina.

It happened so fast. We didn't have time to move or scream.

She grabbed Sabrina and wrapped her fingers around her throat. "DIE! DIIIIIE!" Carly Beth wailed.

Sabrina's eyes bulged. She tried to stagger back. But Carly Beth held on tight. Choking her friend . . . choking her.

Matt and Michael both leaped at Carly Beth. They grabbed her by the shoulders. They struggled to pull her hands off Sabrina's throat.

Carly Beth was a little girl, short and thin. But the two boys couldn't budge her. The evil mask had given her animal strength ... the strength of its evil.

"DIIIIIE! DIIIIIE!"

Sabrina's face turned purple. Her eyelids were half closed. A groan escaped her throat. Her knees buckled.

"Stop! Stop it!" Abby wailed. She threw herself on Carly Beth's back and tried to help Matt and Michael.

Carly Beth twisted and roared like a furious animal.

And suddenly, Sabrina's eyes opened. She pulled herself up straight.

"An ... act ... of ... love," she choked out. "It takes an ... act ... of love."

Standing there helplessly, gripped in horror, I didn't know what Sabrina meant.

But with a startling burst of strength, Sabrina grabbed Carly Beth's wrists. With a desperate groan, she pulled the hands from around her throat.

Then Sabrina grabbed the sides of the ugly green mask. She pulled it toward her — and KISSED Carly Beth on the rutted, cracked, rubbery cheek!

23

Sabrina kissed the disgusting cheek. Then she held on to the head, rubbing it gently, as if caressing it. Soothing it . . .

Carly Beth uttered a soft sigh. Her knees folded. She dropped to the ground.

Sabrina held on to her friend's green, rubbery face, petting the mask. Petting it so tenderly . . .

"It takes an act of love," Sabrina said in a whisper.

And then her fingers dug into the rubbery face — and with a sharp cry, she pulled *up* with all her strength. And TORE the mask off Carly Beth's head.

The mask made a sick, wet sound as it slid off Carly Beth's face. Then, as Sabrina held it high over her head, it opened its mouth in a scream that echoed off the tall hedges.

Sabrina heaved the mask over a hedge. She dropped to her knees and wrapped Carly Beth in a hug.

Carly Beth blinked her eyes and shook her head. She coughed and cleared her throat.

She looked dazed, as if she didn't know where she was.

Finally, she turned to her friend. "Sabrina? Are you okay? Did I hurt you?"

Sabrina nodded. "I knew it wasn't you, Carly Beth. I knew it was the evil of the mask."

"Do you see what's happening?" Michael said. "The monsters from the eggs . . . the Haunted Mask . . . All those things we defeated back home. They followed us here."

"And the only way to get home is to defeat them again?" Matt asked.

No one answered. I guess they were all thinking about the horrors they had faced before.

"We . . . we don't even know if we're going the right way," Julie said, her voice trembling. "We could be going around in circles. And . . . and who *knows* what's waiting for us up ahead!"

"We have no choice," Matt said finally. "We can't turn back. Byron said this maze will lead us to HorrorLand."

"Matt's right," Robby said. "We can't stay here. We know we're in real danger. We have to keep going. Maybe we'll get lucky. Maybe right around the next corner . . ."

His voice faded.

No one else wanted to speak. We started to walk, following the hedges.

Birds cawed overhead. The sky was almost too black to see them. We turned and walked silently down a long, straight passage.

"What time is it?" Jillian asked. "Does anyone have a watch?"

Matt had a watch on a chain on his belt loop. He raised it and squinted at it. "It says midnight," he said.

"Byron told us it's *always* midnight in this maze," Robby said.

We followed the curve in the hedges. Suddenly, the path led steeply downhill. The ground became sandy and soft.

Tall reeds, waving in the breeze, blocked our way. We had to push the reeds aside to make our own path.

Finally, the reeds ended at a sandy shore. "Whoa. Water!" Luke cried.

We stopped at the edge. We were on the shore of a small, round lake. The water was a velvety black under the starless sky. It lapped gently onto the sand at our feet.

"How do we get to the other side?" Michael asked. "Swim?"

Something was tossing out in the water. I heard a splash. A creaking sound.

Squinting hard, I saw a dark shape come into focus.

A ship.

"There's a boat out there," I said. "Can you see it? See the sails moving against the sky?"

We all gazed out over the lake. And as we did, a cover of clouds pulled away from the moon. Pale light washed over the water, and we saw the ship clearly.

An old-fashioned sailing ship with two tall masts. Its sails were unfurled, snapping in the breeze. The boat tilted in the water, rocking gently.

And as the ship came into clear view, we heard voices. Low voices chanting together . . .

"The bones they crack; the bones they creep.
The men come alive in the briny deep.
Come with us; come with the men.
Come meet your fate with Captain Ben."

"Oh, NO!" Billy and Sheena Deep both uttered sharp cries. Their mouths dropped open, and they exchanged quick, frightened glances.

"You were right, Michael," Sheena said. "The horrible things we escaped from before . . . they've followed us to Panic Park."

"We've heard that pirate chant before," Billy said. "We know who that ship belongs to — a pirate who's been dead for two hundred years."

103

"He calls himself Long Ben One-Leg," Sheena said. "He . . . well, let's put it this way — he doesn't like Billy and me."

"This is bad news. We have to go back," Billy said. "We don't want to mess with Captain Ben and his dead pirates."

"We *can't* go back," Matt told Billy. "Do you want to stay here *forever* in this black-and-white world with those creepy shadow people floating around us? We have to get to the other side of this lake."

Lights flickered on the ship. The sails cracked and snapped in the wind. We could hear men's voices. Loud laughter.

A strong gust of wind sent the tall reeds behind us swaying from side to side. They made a creaking sound as the wind pushed them down.

I saw something hidden in the swaying reeds. "Whoa! Check it out!" I cried.

I went running along the shore. My shoes sank into the sand as I ran. The clouds covered the moon again, but I could still see what I had found.

Two longboats. Half buried in the sand. Hidden deep in the reeds.

The other kids hurried over to me. "Look. We can fit eight in a boat. They're perfect," I said.

"No way!" Billy cried. "What do you plan to

do? Row out to the pirate ship? Ask Captain Ben if it's okay to go to the other side?"

The poor guy was shaking. He couldn't hide how frightened he was.

His sister, Sheena, tossed back her dark hair and stared unhappily at the boats. "I . . . don't . . . think . . . so," she said, shaking her head.

"We can row around the lake," I said. "We can stay far away from that pirate ship. Look how dark it is."

"Lizzy is right," Carly Beth said. "We'll sneak around the pirate ship. We'll stay as close to the shore as we can. The pirates will never see us."

Billy and Sheena argued. They didn't want to do it. But they didn't want to be left behind, either.

Finally, they agreed to help.

Working as quietly as we could, we dragged the two longboats into the water. They slid easily from the sandy shore and splashed almost silently into the lake.

Then we piled in — eight to a boat. We just fit. We found the oars in the bottoms of the boats.

Luke and I were at the back of the first boat. I lifted a pair of oars and tested them in the water.

The voices of the men on the ship drifted over the lake. I could hear angry shouts. A loud crash. Then wild laughter.

"They're too busy to look out at the water," I whispered to Luke. "They'll never notice us."

Robby worked his oars in the front of our boat. I rowed from the back.

The narrow boat moved slowly. We were low in the water because of our weight. I had to use all my strength to move us forward.

We kept close to the shore. I could see the reeds bending, swaying in the wind. The cool air felt good on my hot, sweaty face.

I pulled . . . pulled . . . raised the oars and pulled . . .

Suddenly, the boat rocked hard. The bow rose up high, then slapped back down, sending up a spray of lake water.

"Whoa!" Robby whispered from the front. "Something weird is going on!"

"Just row steadily," I said. "Slow and steady."

The wind muffled my voice. I don't know if Robby heard me.

We rocked again. The boat tilted high, then slammed back down with a hard splash.

I leaned over the side of the boat. Beneath us, the water was totally flat and gentle. Why was our boat bucking like a wild bronco?

I turned and glanced back at the second boat. The boat rocked up as if hit by a wave. One of Matt's oars flew out of his hand and splashed into the water.

Our boat roared up again, then crashed down.

Abby cried, "This is CRAZY! Why are we bouncing like this? The water is FLAT!"

I leaned forward into the oars. I tried to concentrate on my rowing. Slow and steady. Slow and steady.

I let out a gasp as I realized the boat had sailed far from the shore.

We rocked up and down, heading toward the center of the lake . . . heading toward the pirate ship.

"Turn it! Turn it!" I called to Robby up front.

"I . . . can't!" he cried. "Lizzy, I can't control it."

I sank my oars in and pulled . . . pulled. Straining to turn the boat back toward the shore.

But Robby was right. We weren't controlling it.

It was like the boat had a mind of its own.

Was it on some kind of track? Was it programmed to sail back to the pirate ship?

Well, that's where we were all heading. Both boats. We rocked wildly up and down — and sailed steadily in a straight line to the ship.

As we moved under the tall ship's cold shadow, I saw the pirates on the deck. There were at least a dozen of them. Most were skeletons wearing dark jackets and ruffled shirts. Their clothes were stained and torn. The rotting shirts barely covered their bones.

Scraggly knots of long hair fell over their empty eye sockets. Clams and seashells clung to their scalps.

They leaned over the rail, watching, white bones glowing in the pale moonlight, ready to greet us.

24

"The bones they crack; the bones they creep.
The men come alive in the briny deep . . ."

The pirates chanted as they pulled us one by one
from the longboats onto their deck. Chanted in
a frightening, slow rhythm. Their voices were
hoarse and dull, the voices of dead men. And I
knew as long as I lived, I'd never forget the terrifying sound.

"Come with us; come with the men.
Come meet your fate with Captain Ben."

The deck rocked gently in the water. We huddled together, staring at the grinning pirates.
Their bones clattered as they moved. Two
of them had purple worms crawling in and out of
their nostril holes. One of them still had some

flesh on his face, sagging skin covered in green mold.

Matt stepped forward. "What do you want?" he demanded. "We're not bothering you. Let us off this ship!"

The dead pirates uttered low grunts but didn't reply. They formed a line to hold us in place. One of them scratched his scraggly hair — and it came off in his hand.

Another pirate started to make choking sounds. I gasped as he coughed up a big half-eaten snail and spit it onto the deck.

"Are you going to let us go?" Matt repeated.

Silence. The boat creaked beneath us.

I could hear the water lapping at the sides. And the hard thumping of my heartbeat.

The chanting voices still rang in my ears. And the dead stare from those deep, empty eye sockets was too horrifying to believe.

I shut my eyes. But the pirates wouldn't go away.

"Can you take us to the other side?" Billy asked in a tiny, frightened voice. "We just want to get to the other side of the lake. Can you take us there?"

The pirates tilted their skulls back and laughed. Dry, choking laughter that sounded more like vomiting than laughing.

They stopped laughing suddenly. I heard

scraping footsteps on the deck behind them. The pirates stumbled and staggered out of the way. They backed to the deck rail, their bones cracking and creaking.

A smiling pirate stepped forward, leaning on a crutch. He had a whole face, but his skin was wrinkled and flaky. As he came closer, I saw that his eyes were watery like poached eggs, and sunken deep in his head.

He wore a long black coat with gold buttons down the front. His sailor pants were nearly in shreds.

His wooden leg tapped the deck as he limped toward us. His thin mustache rose as a smile spread over his face. His teeth were ragged and brown.

"It's Captain Ben," Billy told the rest of us.

The pirate did a low bow. "At your service," he rasped. His voice sounded as if it came from underwater.

His sunken eyes slid over us and stopped at Billy and Sheena. "Well, well, mates — here ye be again!" he boomed.

"Let us go!" Sheena cried. "We're not here to bother you!"

Captain Ben snickered. "Here ye be again," he repeated. His mustache rose up and down like a wriggling worm above his mouth.

"What do you want?" Billy demanded.

The pirate took a step closer. "The Menace promised us revenge," he rasped.

"Who?" Billy and Sheena cried in unison.

"Who is The Menace?" Billy asked.

Captain Ben snickered again. "Too bad you won't live long enough to find out."

25

Leaning on his crutch, Captain Ben walked to the side of the deck. His men scrambled to get out of his way.

His wrinkled skin glowed in the moonlight. He grinned wider and pointed down to a narrow, flat board that stuck out over the edge of the ship.

"The plank," he said. "What would a pirate ship be without a blessed plank — aye, mates?"

One of the pirates began to cough again. He choked up a decayed frog, pulled it out of his open mouth, and tossed it over the rail. I heard the soft splash down below.

"You're all going to walk the plank at midnight," Captain Ben rasped. His mustache slid up at both ends. "And guess what, mates? It's midnight. It's *always* midnight in The Midnight Maze."

The pirates seemed to think that was very funny. They all snickered and coughed and shook their skinless skulls.

"The water be deep here, friends," Captain Ben said, leaning on the rail. "Deep and cold. Too cold to survive for long."

A chill ran down my back. My legs were trembling.

Was he serious? Did he really plan to make us all step off the deck and drop into the water?

I knew the answer. Of *course* he was serious. He was evil. And he was out for revenge.

The word *revenge* repeated in my mind. And in my fright, I began to put some pieces together.

Captain Ben was here for revenge against Billy and Sheena.

What about the Haunted Mask? The monsters from the eggs?

Were they also here for revenge? If they were, who brought them here? Who brought them all here together at the same time?

The same person who invited these Very Special Guests to HorrorLand?

I didn't have any more time to think about it.

Two skeletal pirates grabbed Sheena by the arms. They dragged her across the deck to the plank.

Sheena screamed and tried to break free of the bony hands.

114

But the dead pirates were too strong. They lifted her onto the narrow plank.

Captain Ben raised his wet, eggy eyes to her. "The water be deep here, miss," he said again. "If ye be a good swimmer, you might be able to swim halfway to land before the hungry crocs get you."

Again, the dead pirates laughed and slapped each other as if the captain had made a hilarious joke.

And then the laughter stopped.

Two pirates gave Sheena a shove. She stumbled out onto the plank.

"Please — no!" she begged. "Please —"

"Let my sister go!" Billy screamed. He rushed at Captain Ben. But two pirates quickly blocked his path.

I saw Sheena's knees wobble. She tumbled off the plank — and dropped straight down.

She screamed all the way down.

The splash sent a spray of water over the deck.

I turned and leaned over the rail. I gazed down at the water. Too dark. Too dark to see Sheena.

"Sheena! Sheena!" her brother, Billy, screamed down to her.

Silence. No reply.

Captain Ben tossed his head back and cackled. "Revenge be sweet, mates!" he boomed. "Who be next? How about the young brother here?"

A pirate grabbed Billy.

"No way!" Billy cried. He made a wild grab — and ripped away the pirate's shirt. Pieces of skin clung to the pirate's ribs.

Billy lowered his head and plowed into the dead man's chest. But the pirate didn't crumble or fall. Instead, he wrapped his bony arms around Billy and held him still.

"No! No! No!" Billy screamed, and struggled as the pirates pushed him onto the plank. Another shove — and his hands shot up above his head. His eyes widened in fright. And he went sailing off the end of the board.

Another loud splash sent a spray of water over all of us.

I stared down into the water far below us. I couldn't see anything in the deep blackness.

Captain Ben cackled again. His sunken eyes sparkled with glee.

Abby splashed down next. Then Robby. Then Carly Beth.

I was trembling in fright. I hugged myself to try to stop shaking.

Luke leaned against me. He had tears running down his cheeks. "Lizzy —" he whispered. "Lizzy —"

He was too scared to talk.

I squeezed his hand. "We're good swimmers — right?" I whispered. "We'll swim out of this."

"But — but the pirate said —"

One of the pirates grabbed my brother before he could finish. Luke tried to twist out of his grasp. But he lifted him off the deck and shoved him onto the plank.

I shut my eyes. I couldn't bear to see my little brother fall.

I screamed when I heard the splash.

My scream of horror turned to anger. I balled my hands into fists — and rushed at the laughing pirate captain.

Startled, Captain Ben raised his crutch to shield himself.

I reached to grab it away from him. But two skeletal pirates tackled me and dragged me to the deck.

"No! NOOOOO!" Scream after scream burst from my throat.

And then bony hands lifted me onto the narrow plank.

And pushed me hard.

And I fell screaming into the dark water.

I hit the surface hard, sending up tall waves around me. The slap of the water stung my whole body.

I sucked in a big breath and held it as I sank quickly. The shock of the cold made my arms and legs go stiff.

My heart pounded. I could feel the blood pulsing at my temples.

Total panic. Total panic paralyzed me for a moment.

Then I finally raised my arms. Finally drew in my legs and kicked.

The lake was deeper than I'd thought. By the time I pulled myself to the surface, I was choking and gasping for breath.

Wiping water from my eyes, I gazed around wildly, searching for Luke.

Where was he? Where were the other kids?

Low waves tossed against the side of the pirate

ship. "Hey!" I tried to call out. But panic choked my voice.

"Luke? Where are you? Luke?"

I gazed up at the wooden plank hanging over the deck high above me. I could hear the pirates' raspy voices up there. Laughter. All muffled by the wind and the lapping water.

Everyone fell straight down from the plank. They *had* to be swimming nearby. Where were they?

Where?

"Luke!" I raised my face to the sky and shouted my brother's name again. "Luke — where are you?"

Moonlight shimmered weakly on the dark waters. The lake was empty.

I'm the only one here, I told myself. And the terrifying thought made me want to scream. Or cry.

I'm the only one . . . the only one.

Did the other kids all DROWN?

Sucking in another deep breath, I dove deep underwater. And started to swim away from the shadow of the pirate ship.

Maybe the other kids were all ahead of me, swimming to the other side of the lake. I was the last one off the ship. Maybe I just couldn't see them because they got a head start.

When I came back up to the top, a gust of wind sent a spray of water into my face. Sputtering, I spun around again. I shielded my eyes with my hand and squinted into the pale light.

I saw only the dark, calm water. Pale moonlight flickering on the surface.

No one.

I was all alone.

I opened my mouth to shout again. But before I could get a sound out, I felt a strong pull.

A strong pull from beneath me, pulling me down.

As if a powerful hand had wrapped around me and was tugging me, tugging me under with all its strength.

With a gasp, I flung my arms forward and kicked hard. Tried to pull myself free.

Such a powerful force. I was helpless. Going under.

Being pulled under. Deeper and deeper.

Like being sucked down a drain.

So THIS is what happened to the others!

My last thought before darkness overtook me.

My chest began to ache from holding my breath. I opened my eyes — and saw the muddy lake bottom float into view.

All the way down. I'd been pulled by an intense current all the way down.

In front of me, I gaped at an enormous black hole. A dark rectangle. The water pulled me to it . . . pulled me inside.

A tunnel, I realized. A long, narrow tunnel under the lake.

Did it lead anywhere? Did it lead back to the surface?

It didn't matter. I had no choice. The powerful force had me in its grip. It was pulling me through the underwater passage. Pulling me faster and faster.

If only my lungs could hold out. If only my chest didn't EXPLODE.

All my muscles tensed. I tightened my arms against my sides. And let the current pull me.

The ache from my chest spread over my body. Pain roared down my arms and back and legs. I knew I couldn't hold my breath much longer.

And then a deafening *WHOOSH* startled me. I felt a strong push from behind.

And I went shooting up. I soared up through the narrow tunnel — and burst out of the water.

My breath came spilling out. Raising my head over the water, I sucked in breath after breath, wheezing, gasping hoarsely, my chest still throbbing.

I shook my head and wiped the water from my eyes. I spun around, struggling to see where I was.

"Hey —" Did I hear a voice?

I looked up — and saw someone waving to me from the dark shore. And then two other kids. And then some others pulling themselves from the water, stepping shakily onto the land.

"Luke!" I cried. "Luke!"

He was still in the water, up to his waist. I splashed over to him. "You're okay!" I cried.

"I . . . guess so," he said, his voice cracking. "I guess we made it, Lizzy."

I grabbed his hand and helped pull him onto the sandy shore. "We made it! We made it!" I shouted.

The others all gathered around, shivering and shaking off water. I counted heads — sixteen of us. Everyone.

"We're ALIVE! ALIVE!" Michael cried, thrusting his fists above his head.

We didn't celebrate for long. We were too cold and wet. I felt exhausted, more tired than I'd ever felt.

I shivered. It wasn't just the cold — it was also my fear.

Hugging myself, I turned to the water. I could see the hulking blackness of the pirate ship, tilting in the middle of the lake.

"We're on the other side of the lake," Carly Beth said, squeezing water from her hair. "That underwater tunnel must be part of the maze. It brought us to where we wanted to go."

I turned and saw the walls of tall hedges. "That must be where the maze continues," I said.

"Maybe we're near the end," Abby said wearily. "I . . . I'm so tired. I don't know how much longer . . ." Her words ended in a sob.

Julie hugged her. "We'll help each other," she told Abby. "We'll get through this maze. Byron said we could do it. And he said it would lead us back to HorrorLand."

Without another word, we turned and started to follow the path between the hedges. Luke and

I walked side by side, keeping our eyes straight ahead.

"We've been in this maze for hours," he murmured. "It has to end soon — doesn't it?"

"I hope so," I said. "I . . . I'm never going to another scary movie as long as I live!"

That made Luke laugh. "Yeah. And no more scary books or scary video games!" he said.

We both laughed.

"When we get home, we'll spend all our time watching *SpongeBob* and the Disney Channel," Luke said. "From now on —"

"Wait, Luke —" I said. I held him back and pointed. "Look — is that the end of the maze?"

"Whoa!"

"Check it out!"

We all stopped. The hedge walls ended a few yards in front of us. And beyond them, we could see bright gray light.

Warm air floated in from the wide opening at the end of the hedges. I took a long, deep breath. And then I started to run with the others.

As we came bursting out of the maze, a large black-and-white sign came into view. Actually, it was a big banner, spread across a brick wall.

In big, bold letters, the banner read: **WELCOME TO HORRORLAND!**

We all cheered and screamed. We jumped up and down and slapped high fives and pumped our fists in the air in triumph.

I hugged Luke. We cheered and laughed.

Over Luke's shoulder, I saw five or six big Horrors thundering toward us.

"Yes! Yes!" I screamed happily. "We made it! We're BACK!"

28

The green-and-purple Horrors roared up to us, their big feet slapping the pavement. Their furry chests were bare under the dark overalls they wore. Curled horns poked up from their heads and caught the glare of the bright light.

We stopped cheering. The Horrors didn't look like a welcoming committee.

Their eyes were narrowed coldly on us. Their faces were set in scowls and ugly frowns.

As they came near, they formed a line. They spread their big arms, as if ready to grab us or keep us from escaping.

"Hey — we came back!" Matt shouted.

"We're back in HorrorLand!" Carly Beth exclaimed.

The Horrors didn't answer. They scowled at us in silence.

Suddenly, I knew that something was very wrong.

The Horrors were in color, all purple and green. But as I glanced around, I saw that the rest of the park was in black and white. All shades of black and gray.

I pointed to the wall. "The banner —" I said to the Horrors. "We're back in HorrorLand — right? It says we're back in HorrorLand."

Some of the Horrors laughed.

"That's his idea of a joke," one of them muttered.

"He has a twisted sense of humor," another Horror said. He sneered. "You'll find out soon enough."

I gasped. "You mean — we're still in Panic Park?"

"Who are you talking about?" Carly Beth demanded. "*Who* has a twisted sense of humor?"

"Yeah. Who put up that banner?" Matt asked.

The Horrors didn't answer. They stood in their tight line, staring at us coldly.

"What do you want?" Matt asked. "Tell us. Why are you guarding us? What are you going to do to us?"

They didn't move or speak.

I felt a wave of panic roll down my body. I shuddered.

After a long silence, Matt turned to Jillian. "They won't talk. But you can read their minds — right?"

Jillian faced one of the Horrors, a tall creature with yellow fur on top of his green head.

"Go ahead," Matt urged. "Quick. Read his mind. What do they plan to do?"

Jillian squinted up at the Horror and concentrated hard.

He stared back at her without moving.

A few seconds passed. Then Jillian stepped back.

"I . . . I can't," she stammered. "They're Horrors. They're not human. I can't read their thoughts."

I let out a sharp cry.

I grabbed Jillian by the shoulders. "Jillian, how could you DO that to all of us?" I screamed.

She snatched my wrists and shoved my hands away. "What are you talking about?" she cried.

"You *lied*!" I shouted. "You are a LIAR!"

She blinked at me. "Lizzy, you're crazy! You're totally crazy!"

"No," I insisted. "You told us you could read Byron's mind — remember? When he showed up here and took us to The Midnight Maze. We asked you to read his thoughts. We asked if he was telling the truth."

"So?" Jillian sneered at me.

"You said you read Byron's mind. You told us Byron was telling the truth," I said. "You said we could trust Byron. But Byron is a Horror.

And *now* you say you can't read Horrors' minds."

"Well . . ." Jillian's cheeks turned red. She took a step back.

"You're a total liar!" I repeated. I moved toward her angrily. "You lied about me. And you lied about Byron. Why?" ●

Jackson stepped between us. "Give Jillian a break," he said. "Get out of my sister's face."

Matt gave Jackson a hard shove — and knocked Jackson onto his back. "You're *both* liars — aren't you!" Matt said. "We thought you were our friends. Why did you trick us? Why did you do this to us?"

Jillian's face became more flushed. She had tears in her eyes. She shook her head hard, as if she was confused. "I — I —" she stammered.

Then suddenly the Horrors backed up. I turned in time to see a man step out from behind them.

He wore a black suit and a black shirt. His face was hidden in the shadow of a wide-brimmed black hat.

"Go ahead — fight!" he said in a booming, deep voice. "Mix it up. Go ahead, Lizzy. You're right. Jillian lied to you. Jillian is a liar! Tear her hair. Come on — rip her eyes out! Let's go, everyone! Let's fight! I love this! Don't you just LOVE it?"

29

I struggled to see the man's face. But he kept it well hidden under the brim of the black hat.

Staring hard, I realized he was completely covered in black. He wore a black tie over his black shirt. He even had black gloves over his hands.

I backed away from Jillian.

Jackson climbed to his feet and huddled beside his sister.

We all stared in silence at the man with the booming voice.

"No one wants to mix it up? No one wants to give me a good fight? Show me some blood?"

He sounded truly disappointed.

"We just want to know where we are," Matt said. "And what's going on here."

"Let me welcome you," the man said. "I hope you enjoyed your first little test in Panic Park."

"Test?" Michael cried. "What kind of test?"

"You did very well," the man said, ignoring Michael's question. "Very well indeed. I enjoyed seeing you tremble in fear. Your fear was very real. That's what we want. REAL fear! And I liked the way you dealt with it. Very impressive."

"This dude is way weird," Luke whispered to me. "Is he *joking*?"

"I wish," I muttered.

"I already knew you were brave," the man continued. "That's why you were all chosen. And you showed a lot of courage in The Midnight Maze. But that was baby stuff."

He chuckled. "Now we'll see how brave you are when it REALLY starts to get scary!"

Some kids gasped.

I felt my heart skip a beat.

Panic Park had been *terrifying* from the moment we arrived. Why was he talking about making it *scarier*?

"Who are you?" Michael shouted. "Are we supposed to be scared of you because you're all dressed in black? Why don't you give us a break and tell us what you want."

The man touched the brim of his hat. "My name is Karloff Mennis," he said. "Most people call me The Menace."

My heart skipped again. I had a sudden heavy feeling in my stomach.

The Menace. We had heard that name before.

"I am your host here," he said. "I built this park. I brought you here for a reason. I need a favor. Just one little favor, that's all."

"A favor from *us*?" Carly Beth cried.

He nodded.

"If we do it, can we go home?" Carly Beth asked.

"Well . . . that's just it," The Menace replied, lowering his voice. "The simple favor is *this* . . . I need you to stay here in Panic Park — FOREVER!"

To be continued in . . .

#12 THE STREETS OF PANIC PARK

INSPECTOR CRANIUM
THOUGHT POLICE

Can Read
mind of anyone
over the age of three,
except for Horrors, who
always have the mind of a two-year-old

Can use
brainpower
to open bottles
and cans.

WHEN IN DOUBT: Empty out a brain,
ask questions later!

FAQs – Freakishly Absurd Questions About The Vampire State Building

Located in Vampire Village at the intersection of Hollywood & Vein, The Vampire State Building is the tallest structure in HorrorLand.

Q: How Can I Find the Vampire State Building?

A: Follow the Yellow Guano Road. Don't try asking any vampires for directions — they can be a pain in the neck!

Q: What's inside?

A: PLASMA PLAZA, shops like FANGS FOR THE MEMORIES ANTIQUES, and restaurants like DRACULA'S STAKE HOUSE. The upper floors have BAT-ting cages and a 6-scream movie theater with all-coffin seating.

Q: Can I go to the top?

A: Yes! Our observation deck is open every night from sundown to sunrise and offers a one-of-a-kind view of HorrorLand. All we ask is a small donation from each guest (one or two pints, depending on your size).

Q: Why are all the windows blacked out?

A: Please hurry over so we can answer that question for you in person!

THE COFFIN CRUISE

WORM BAIT

Connects to Map # 9

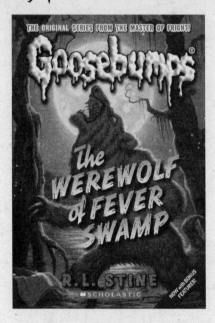

We moved to Florida during Christmas vacation. A week later, I heard the frightening howls in the swamp for the first time.

Night after night, the howls made me sit up in bed. I would hold my breath and wrap my arms around myself to keep from shivering.

I would stare out my bedroom window at the chalk-colored full moon. And I would listen.

What kind of creature makes such a cry? I would ask myself.

And how close is it? Why does it sound as if it's right outside my window?

The wails rose and fell like police car sirens. They weren't sad or mournful. They were menacing.

Angry.

They sounded to me like a warning. *Stay out of the swamp. You do not belong here.*

When my family first moved to Florida, to our new house at the edge of the swamp, I couldn't wait to explore. I stood in the backyard with the binoculars my dad had given me for my twelfth birthday and gazed toward the swamp.

Trees with slender white trunks tilted over each other. Their flat, broad leaves appeared to form a roof, covering the swamp floor in blue shadow.

Behind me, the deer paced uneasily in their wire-mesh pen. I could hear them pawing the soft, sandy ground, rubbing their antlers against the walls of their pen.

Lowering my binoculars, I turned to look at them. The deer were the reason we had moved to Florida.

You see, my dad, Michael F. Tucker, is a scientist. He works for the University of Vermont in Burlington, which, believe me, is a *long* way from the Florida swamps!

Dad got these six deer from some country in South America. They're called swamp deer. They're not like regular deer. I mean, they don't look like Bambi. For one thing, their fur is very red, not brown. And their hooves are really big and kind of webbed. For walking on wet, swampy ground, I guess.

Dad wants to see if these South American swamp deer can survive in Florida. He plans to put little radio transmitters on them and set them free in the swamp. Then he'll study how they get along.

When he told us back in Burlington that we were moving to Florida because of the deer, we all totally freaked. We didn't want to move.

My sister, Emily, cried for days. She's sixteen, and she didn't want to miss her senior year in high school. I didn't want to leave my friends, either.

But Dad quickly got Mom on his side. Mom is a scientist, too. She and Dad work together on a lot of projects. So, of course, she agreed with him.

And the two of them tried to persuade Emily and me that this was the chance of a lifetime, that it was going to be really exciting. An adventure we'd never forget.

So here we were, living in a little white house in a neighborhood of four or five other little white houses. We had six weird-looking red deer penned up behind the house. The hot Florida sun was beaming down. And an endless swamp stretched beyond our flat, grassy backyard.

I turned away from the deer and raised the binoculars to my face. "Oh," I cried out as two dark eyes seemed to be staring back at me.

I pulled the binoculars away and squinted toward the swamp. In the near distance I saw a large white bird on two long, spindly legs.

"It's a crane," Emily said. I hadn't realized Emily had stepped up beside me. She was wearing a sleeveless white T-shirt and short red denim shorts. My sister is tall and thin and very blond. She looks a lot like a crane.

The bird turned and began high-stepping toward the swamp.

"Let's follow it," I said.

Emily made her pouting face, an expression we'd all seen a lot of since moving down here. "No way. It's too hot."

"Aw, come on." I tugged her skinny arm. "Let's do some exploring, check out the swamp."

She shook her head, her white-blond ponytail swinging behind her. "I really don't want to, Grady." She adjusted her sunglasses on her nose. "I'm kind of waiting for the mail."

Since we're so far from the nearest post office, we only get mail two times a week. Emily had been spending most of her time waiting for the mail.

"Waiting for a love letter from Martin?" I asked with a grin. She hated when I teased her about Martin, her boyfriend back in Burlington. So I teased her as often as I could.

"Maybe," she said. She reached out with both hands and messed up my hair. She knows I hate to have my hair messed up.

"Please?" I pleaded. "Come on, Emily. Just a short walk. Very short."

"Emily, take a short walk with Grady," Dad's voice broke in. We turned to see him inside the deer pen. He had a clipboard in one hand and was going from deer to deer, taking notes. "Go ahead," he urged my sister. "You're not doing anything else."

"But, Dad —" Emily could whine with the best of them when she wanted.

"Go ahead, Em," Dad insisted. "It will be interesting. More interesting than standing around in the heat, arguing with him."

Emily pushed the sunglasses up again. They kept slipping down her nose. "Well . . ."

"Great!" I cried. I was really excited. I'd never been in a real swamp before. "Let's go!" I grabbed my sister's hand and pulled.

Emily reluctantly followed, a fretful expression on her face. "I have a bad feeling about this," she muttered.

My shadow slanting behind me, I hurried toward the low, tilting trees. "Emily, what could go wrong?" I asked.

About the Author

R.L. Stine's books are read all over the world. So far, his books have sold more than 300 million copies, making him one of the most popular children's authors in history. Besides Goosebumps, R.L. Stine has written the teen series Fear Street and the funny series Rotten School, as well as the Mostly Ghostly series, The Nightmare Room series, and the two-book thriller *Dangerous Girls*. R.L. Stine lives in New York with his wife, Jane, and Minnie, his King Charles spaniel. You can learn more about him at www.RLStine.com.

PLACE ON EARTH!

The Original Bone-Chilling

Goosebumps® Series

THIS BOOK IS YOUR TICKET TO

www.EnterHorrorLand.com

CHECKLIST #11

ESCAPE FROM HORRORLAND
R.L. STINE
SCHOLASTIC

☐ Take a spin on the Coffin Cruise—but WATCH OUT for those rusty nails.

☐ ELIMINATE the glowing red eyes in Vampire Village.

☐ Spiders and lice and wee little mice... Were you expecting burgers and fries? UNCOVER what vampires are REALLY made of.

☐ JOURNEY to the top of the Vampire State Building for a BITING good time.

UNLOCK THE 11ᵀᴴ MAP!

_____

USER NAME

_____

PASSWORD

For more frights, check out the Goosebumps HorrorLand video game!

SCHOLASTIC